J
Jones, C
A CAT CALLED
CAMOUFLAGE

7/9 3

AUG 22 '72 DELANO			
NOV 1 2 '80	S, W"		

Ruth, whose mother and father have quarreled themselves into a separation, is now living with her unhappy mother in a strange town and wondering if she will ever make friends with the children in her new school. Wondering too how important friends are. Wondering what makes her unpredictable mother tick.

Ruth does find friends. First she meets a curious and adverturous cat she calls Camouflage, and through Camouflage, Michael, the boy who plays the violin at school and who lives on the farm just outside of town. Then Camouflage's mistress, Miss Barnaby, the reclusive spinster who lives all alone in the big house, invites her to tea.

Soon, Ruth finds a way of using her days that pleases her. As the weeks pass, she learns a great deal about herself, and about other people. And Ruth's mother changes, too. She is no stereotype mama, but a real person who learns and grows along with Ruth. By the end of the book Ruth and her family, and the reader, as well, know something about patterns of living that break apart because they do not meet the needs of the people who live by them, and about ways of forming hopeful new patterns through compromise and honesty and love.

A CAT CALLED CAMOUFLAGE

A CAT CALLED CAMOUFLAGE
Cordelia Jones

Illustrated by the author

S. G. PHILLIPS *New York*

Contents

A CAT CALLED CAMOUFLAGE

1

First meeting

Mrs Renton says I encouraged Camouflage. 'I can't have your Ruth encouraging stray cats into my house, Mrs Wintersgill,' she said to my mother. But that isn't so. You can't call it 'encouraging' just if you happen to stop to talk to a cat, and a very conversational cat at that, whom you happen to meet from time to time. In fact, I actually *dis*couraged her just as soon as she started following me. Mrs Renton can't expect me never to talk to a cat in the street just because she's such a mean old woman that she can't abide cats.

This is how it all started:

I first saw Camouflage – or rather, at first I did not see her – lying in a rose bed in a front garden in Blossomgate on my way back from school. She was washing herself. Camouflage is not an ordinary tabby; she is brindled all over her body the colour of a wild rabbit, rather darker along the spine and with some dark spots arranged very beautifully on her creamy stomach. There are stripes on her legs and also on her tail, and her face is very pointed with the most enormous ears. Each ear is very pointed too, and at the tip it is finished off with a little quiff of hair which gives her a rather wild look, not like the ordinarily stolid domesticated cat. Her colouring makes it almost impossible to see her at times, which is why I called her Camouflage; I did think of calling her 'The Speaker' because she is such a conversational cat, but she seemed to recognise 'Camouflage' much better, almost as if it really was her name, so Camouflage she became.

This first time I saw her I almost didn't see her, and it was only because she moved that I saw her at all. And then, naturally, I stopped and watched her. She soon noticed I was watching her and, tossing back her head, greeted me with a rather affronted miaow, as if to say, 'Have you never seen a cat washing herself before? Have you no better manners than to stand and stare like that?' However, after very thoroughly washing her face she decided to make my acquaintance. She strolled over and jumped on the garden wall, and, talking all the time, rubbed herself against me and got herself stroked. She had an outsize purr for such a small cat and I could hardly bring myself to leave her. She was so pleased to have found a new friend. And when at last I did manage to leave her I felt very lonely and sad going back to Mrs Renton's dreadful catless house.

You see, we used to have a cat. That was when we lived in a house of our own, before Daddy left us. Now we live in lodgings and Mrs Renton is our landlady. Our cat was called Byron and he was a great big black tom. I was very fond of him and when I was little I used to tell him all my troubles, because there was no one much else who would listen, but Byron would sit there sympathetically winking an eye and purring, though sometimes it was difficult to prevent him from falling asleep. When we came here, and Mrs Renton wouldn't have cats, Mummy said he would have to be destroyed. I was aghast, but luckily I persuaded our daily woman, Mrs Raines, to take him. I believe he is very happy and comfortable living with the Raineses and doesn't miss me at all. It is I who miss him. I haven't made any friends in Knaresley and I wish I had Byron here to talk to.

At first when Daddy left us I thought it wasn't going to make much difference. We went on living at Horsepath, and anyway he was never much at home even before he left us. He is a traveller for a Leeds firm and so he was away most of the time. Mummy was always complaining about his being away but when he did come home she was always in such a filthy temper with him that I don't blame him if he didn't come home as often as he could have done. When he was at home she always found something to quarrel about. Sometimes it was something so grown up that I couldn't make out what it was about, like the time when I was quite little and my mother sat on the stairs and cried for about half an hour and Mrs Raines took me out into the kitchen and said, 'There, never you mind, my duck. Your mother's just a bit upset, that's all.' But more recently they used to quarrel about money, that I do know, but all the whys and wherefores I knew nothing of; and then they used to quarrel about the stupidest things – any child would have known better. For instance, the time about the coffee. Daddy didn't take sugar in his coffee. Mummy always poured out the coffee at breakfast and this time she put sugar in. I don't suppose she put it in on purpose. Nobody ever suggested she put it in on purpose. Daddy just said, 'You've put sugar in this coffee, Margaret.'

'Oh,' she said, 'then why don't you pour your own coffee?'

Daddy didn't say anything, but he drew a deep breath of exasperation, and that was enough. When Mummy loses her temper, the sound of her voice changes. She does not go red, instead she goes very white and taut.

'How do you expect me to remember whether you take sugar or not. If you treat this place as a hotel at least have the decency to treat me with the same civility as you would the hotel servants. You expect me to get up and make you your breakfast, set the table, serve it, wash it up and – AND you expect me to know whether you take sugar in your beastly coffee. I've had enough of this, let me tell you . . .'

This sort of thing used to happen more and more frequently until one day Daddy wrote to say he would never be coming back again. I don't blame him for that either, really, only I wish he had taken me with him. I did say to my mother, couldn't I go and live with him, or at least for some of the time; but he doesn't want me, or so my mother says. I think he might have written to me, if he loved me at all; but he didn't write, even for my birthday.

So we went on living in Horsepath, my mother and I, and Byron too. And then one day I happened to be talking to her about what we were going to be doing in school the next year and whom we were going to have for form mistress when suddenly she said, 'That won't matter to you. You won't be going to that school any more.'

I looked at her with my mouth open and asked what she meant.

Mummy always expects you to know things she has never told you about and then gets very cross when she has to explain them to you. 'You don't expect us to go on living in this barrack, do you?' she exclaimed. 'Do you expect me to spend all the rest of my life doing housework from morning till night?'

'No,' I said. She was always complaining about having to do housework, though she had Mrs Raines to help her. (She was always complaining about Mrs Raines too, though really Mrs Raines was very nice and Byron would have had to be destroyed if it hadn't been for her.) We did live in a big house, it's true; she always calls it 'that barrack'.

So then Mummy explained to me that she'd got a job in Knaresley, teaching at the Modern School and we were going to come and live here. It's funny to think that in those days 'Knaresley' was just a name I'd seen on the fronts of buses, and now I live here.

I first saw Knaresley a little after I'd heard about all this, when we came over to look for rooms. It was dreadful weather, raining all the time. We got soaked. We had lunch in a place called the Cosy Café, which is the sort that serves you mashed potatoes, grey in colour, in little round balls like ice-cream, and the cloth was stained with gravy. Now that I live in Knaresley, when I pass that café, I always think of that time when the place was all strange and I try to remember what it seemed like then.

It isn't a bad town really. It stands just at the entrance to Knaresdale and over the housetops one can see the lonely fells rising, which is much better than Horsepath which, being a suburb, has nothing but houses wherever you look. But that first day the fells were blotted out by the rain and all I can remember is going from one dreadful house to another and being told to wipe my feet on innumerable door mats. Now I know the town I can identify some of the places we went to, and I know Knaresley is not a very big place; then it seemed endless and all the same, street after street of gaunt, unwelcoming houses. Why we chose Mrs Renton's I do not know. None of the others can have been worse. Perhaps they were more expensive. I wonder if any of them would have allowed cats.

Mrs Renton's house is in a terrace on Station Road. At the front it is built of shiny yellow brick with red stripes and it has gothic windows which make the rooms inside very dark. At the back it is built of grey brick and has ordinarily shaped windows. We have the rooms on the first floor. The sitting-room is at the front and the main advantage is that there is a balcony outside the window because the room below has a bow window sticking out. In front of the house is a bit of garden composed of gravel in which grows a plum tree, very ancient, which leans towards our balcony. 'There are never any plums on it,' said Mrs Renton to me, 'so you won't be able to steal them.' From the front door to the gate is a path of red and blue tiles and to show you the sort of person Mrs Renton is I tell you that she *washes* it almost every day. I think she would like me not to walk on it.

At the back of the house is another garden which is kept so neat that scarcely anything grows there except a number of apple trees which Mrs Renton is thinking of cutting down because children steal the apples. There is also a shed in which I keep my bicycle and a door into the back lane. When I leave my bicycle there I have to walk round the end of the terrace and come in at the front door because otherwise I would have to go through Mrs Renton's kitchen and sitting-room. We are supposed to be able to go through her rooms to reach the dustbin once a week but I never have. Mummy does. Nevertheless I have been in her room. You can imagine the sort of room it is with lots of ornaments and antimacassars. She has a piano there but I don't think she ever plays it and on the piano is a framed photograph of Mrs Renton and Mr Renton (who is dead) at their wedding, and another one of him alone. He looks rather amiable, but then even Mrs Renton looks quite pleasant in her wedding photo so you can't tell. I wonder what he was like. His name was Harold, I found out, though she always refers to him as Mr Renton, and whenever she is being particularly unreasonable she says Mr Renton would back her up, if he were alive, poor man. Mummy says she'd bet anything he wouldn't, but not to Mrs Renton, of course.

The other thing I noticed in Mrs Renton's room was the cyclamen plants. She has two or three but they never flower for her so she has some plastic cyclamen flowers which she sticks in amongst the real leaves. I had a good look: the plants are real, but the flowers are plastic.

There is one more thing I ought to tell you about Mrs Renton and her house and that is The Great Picture Row. When we first came here Mummy took down all the pictures hanging in our rooms because she didn't like them.

'That looks better,' she said, standing back when she had taken them down. 'Even the pale patches on the walls are better than those horrors. If I go over to Horsepath I'll bring one or two pictures back with me to brighten the place up.'

We found some space in a cupboard where we could stow most of them away. In there we put the drawing of Fountains Abbey by a local artist.

'I can't read his name,' said my mother, squinting at the signature, 'but he ought to learn to draw.'

And next we put in the thatched cottage with hollyhocks.

'Pure chocolate box,' said my mother.

And then there was just room for the reproduction of a vase of flowers made to look all lumpy as if it were real paint, at which my mother said nothing; she only made a face. Which left us with the largest picture of all, an old oil-painting of dead pheasants which you could scarcely see because it was so dark.

'The frame alone would fill the whole wardrobe,' Mummy

said disgustedly. She turned its face to the wall. 'I suppose someone could use those stretchers.'

'But it's Mrs Renton's,' I said.

'Oh, I know, I'm not proposing to do anything to it. Though why anyone should wish to preserve it I can't imagine.'

It was still leaning against the wall when Mrs Renton came in to ask if we had everything we wanted. The bare patch above the mantelpiece was the first thing she noticed.

'Oh dear,' she said, 'has that fallen down again? I believe I've got some more picture wire downstairs.' She sounded cross and I daresay she was thinking, 'That's the first thing they've broken.'

'There's nothing wrong with the wire,' said my mother brightly. 'It's the picture I don't like.'

There was an awkward pause.

'It's a very valuable painting, Mrs Wintersgill. It's an original oil-painting and very old. Very old indeed.'

'Victorian, I should guess,' said my mother, making an effort to sound polite.

'As I was saying, very old indeed,' said Mrs Renton icily. 'It belonged to my grandmother. I believe it should be in a museum.'

'What a pity it isn't,' said my mother, still making herself sound polite. 'It's rather dark and gloomy to live with.'

'I'll get some more picture wire,' said Mrs Renton grimly.

'But there's nothing wrong with the picture wire. I took the picture down myself.'

'Then you will kindly put it up again.'

'But Mrs Renton, we have to live in these rooms. That picture . . .'

'I never heard of such a thing . . .'

'. . . will be perfectly safe in the wardrobe.'

14

'If Mr Renton was alive, I don't know what he would think.'

'I assure you, Mrs Renton . . .'

'He never would have allowed it. Who does this house belong to, I should like to know?'

'Of course, Mrs Renton, but we have to live in these rooms. I . . .'

'Next you'll be throwing my furniture out into the street!'

'But I'm not throwing this picture out into the street!'

By now Mrs Renton had noticed the absence of the other pictures. 'I suppose you've already thrown them out into the street.'

'This is becoming ridiculous!' My mother no longer sounded polite.

'I'm afraid you'd better start looking for somewhere else to live, if that is your attitude.'

'I most certainly shall!'

But when Mrs Renton had gone, my mother said, 'I suppose we'd better put them up again,' and when she faced the original oil-painting round again, 'Valuable, my hat! The ignorant old fool!' But she went down and patched it up with Mrs Renton.

There are two other pictures I should like to mention. They hang on the stairs leading up to our rooms and they are both brown dingy reproductions. One shows a little boy in frilly clothes standing on a stool in the middle of a big room and round a table are a whole lot of stern men in black clothes and black hats. Underneath is the title which says, 'When did you last see your father?' One day Mummy caught me looking at it and she said rather angrily, 'If Mrs Renton were a little more intelligent I'd think she'd put that there on purpose. She's spiteful enough.' After that I never dared look at the picture if either Mummy or Mrs Renton was around; I turn my head the other way when I get to that point on the stairs.

The other picture on the staircase is called *The Old Shepherd's Chief Mourner*. There is a coffin standing in a room, the Old Shepherd's coffin, and the chief mourner is his faithful old sheepdog who is sitting by the coffin resting his head on it, just as a dog will put his chin on your knee if he wants a bit of love and affection. I thought it was very sad but Mummy told me it was 'frightfully sentimental'. 'I can't stand people who call animals "Our Dumb Friends" ' she said; 'people who think dogs and cats have all the same feelings as human beings – all the good and noble feelings, that is, not the nasty ones. Don't you go getting sentimental about Byron,' she added; 'he won't come and weep at your bier.' (She did not need to tell me that.)

I bring all this up because I don't want you to think that I am sentimental about Camouflage either. She is a dear sweet cat but the things that she does in this book she did for her own amusement, out of curiosity, or because she was hungry, not because she was noble and brave, or loving and loyal.

2

A cat in the house

After I'd first seen Camouflage I used to look out for her, because she was a Cat of Character. Not only did she look different, but also she was much more talkative than other cats. I saw her once or twice and we had a chat and the second time she tried to follow me but I managed to discourage her. She started chasing a leaf and lost interest in me, and I was able to hurry off without her noticing. I remember coming home just a week after our first meeting; I did not see her in her usual street, but then, when I arrived at Mrs Renton's house, there she was, sitting on the garden wall looking terribly smug and pleased with herself as if to say, 'Look, I've discovered where you live.'

I stopped and talked to her and asked her what she was doing so far from home and petted her a bit. Then I went up the garden path. She followed me.

'Look, puss, you must go home,' I said.

She only rubbed herself against my legs and then, running up to the door, miaowed to be let in, rubbing her head against the door and looking up at me beseechingly, mewing, and purring in between times.

'It is no good, Camouflage,' I said. 'Mrs Renton doesn't like cats, and besides what will your own people say when they find you're missing?'

But it was no good talking to her; she took no notice. In the end I took her back to her own street – that is, the street where I'd seen her before. But she wouldn't be left. Every time I tried to slip away home she followed me. I didn't like to knock on anyone's door to ask if she was their cat, because I'd no idea which house she lived in. At last, when I was almost despairing, she disappeared. I couldn't see her anywhere, so I hurried off home, looking over my shoulder every step or two to see I wasn't followed. I reached Mrs Renton's in safety, or so I thought. I had just taken out my key when there she was, on the doorstep, purring and mewing, her nose to the crack of the door, ready to slip through as soon as it was opened. I tore my hair. 'You incorrigible cat!' I exclaimed. (That is one of our form-mistress's words.)

I picked her up, opened the door, stepped inside, dumped her outside and shut the door. It was all done in a trice. I felt awful, but what else could I do?

I went upstairs, into the front room, and looked out of the window. I couldn't see the doorstep because of our balcony and I didn't like to open the window for fear of attracting her attention. But presently I saw her walking down the path; she had given up hope. She jumped on to the garden wall and began to wash. Sadly I pressed my nose against the window pane (it left a greasy mark which Mummy made me clean off afterwards). 'If only you could understand,' I thought, addressing Camouflage, 'that I don't want to be unkind or inhospitable. I should love you to come in here, but Mrs Renton would make a row. Besides, you have a home of your own, I expect.'

Unfortunately she saw me suddenly. She stopped in the midst of her washing and flung me an indignant but delighted miaow. She jumped down from the wall into the garden and began to sharpen her claws on the plum tree. I stepped hastily back into the room to be out of sight. But suddenly she shot up the tree; when she reached the branching of the boughs she stopped to look around, saw me inside the room and came out along the branch that came nearest to our balcony. There she stopped and mewed. I could not bear to leave the room. What would she do next?

She crouched ready to jump, then thought better of it and mewed indignantly. She tried to get further along the branch and decided it was not safe. She went back to the trunk and tried another branch, which was no better. She retreated backwards along it, and returned to her original position. She mewed piteously.

'I can't help you, my dear Camouflage,' I said miserably, 'and anyway you can't come in.'

Again she crouched. The branch did not come very near the balcony. I held my breath. This time she jumped. Of course, since then she has jumped from the plum tree to the balcony and vice versa hundreds of times and thinks nothing of it, but that first time my heart missed a beat. I went straight to the window and let her in. 'You naughty cat, you incorrigible cat, you mustn't do things like that,' I said, stroking and kissing her.

As soon as she was inside the room Camouflage was all curiosity. She went about on tiptoe as it were, her eyes wide, her nose twitching and her ears pricked. She looked behind everything, under everything and on top of everything. She tried all the cupboard doors and she got inside the waste-paper basket. Meanwhile I went to fetch her a saucer of milk. She was still drinking it when my mother came in. (I always get home before her.)

I was afraid Mummy would be cross but she wasn't. She really likes cats, you know. What she said about Byron being destroyed wasn't like her at all; she was in a bad temper at the time. All she said now was, 'You shouldn't have given her that milk. She'll come again. She looks quite sharp enough to run two homes at once and get fed twice over.'

Camouflage stayed with us until after tea. Then, since Mrs Renton was not around, I took her downstairs and put her out of the front door. She made no objection, but trotted off quite happily. So that's the end of that, I thought. Perhaps she'll come again. It would be nice if she paid us an occasional visit. With a cat in my lap even Mrs Renton's rooms felt like home.

That night, I hadn't been in bed very long when my mother peeped round the door. 'Are you asleep?' she asked.

'No.'

'It's that cat of yours. She came up the plum tree and asked to be let in at the window.'

I sat up in bed. 'Where is she?'

Camouflage came running into the room, released from my mother's arms, and jumped on the bed, purring and nuzzling up against me.

'You shouldn't have given her that milk,' my mother said. Presently she crept downstairs and put Pussy out of the front door again.

The next morning when I went into the front room and drew the curtains, what should I see on the balcony! She had evidently been there some time as she was settled, dozing quite comfortably on the parapet. The noise of the curtains awoke her and she demanded to be let in.

At first my mother wouldn't let me give her any milk, but in the end her heart melted and she gave her some herself. Camouflage was ravenous. She fell upon a piece of bread that I dropped by accident, and ate it all up.

'Look how hungry she is, Mummy,' I said.

'Never believe a cat,' said my mother. 'They are very wily creatures, quite capable of eating a good dinner and then going round to the neighbours to complain that they're half starved.'

When we left for school, pussy went with us. She followed us almost all the way. She did not leave us when we reached the street where I thought she lived. It was not until we met a dog coming along the pavement that she took refuge in somebody's garden, and after that I didn't see her again.

When I got back from school she was sitting up the plum tree.

'This is getting to be too much of a good thing,' said my mother when she came in. (I did not tell her that I had given Camouflage a big plate of bread and milk which she had devoured in record time.) 'We must take her back to her own home.'

After tea we put her in the basket that had been Byron's and took her down to the street where I had first seen her. There we took her from house to house. No one had seen her before. No one knew whose she was. We tried some houses in neighbouring streets. At last we let Camouflage out of the basket.

'Perhaps she'll find her own way home,' Mummy said.

Camouflage wandered off.

'There, what did I tell you?' said Mummy.

When we got back she was sitting up the plum tree.

3

No road for motors

A little way along Station Road is a shop on a corner which calls itself 'The Corner Shop' and is kept by a kind old lady called Mrs Cousins. Outside the door is a glass covered notice board and if you pay you can put a notice on it. Mummy wrote out a notice to put there which ran 'FOUND: a small speckled brown cat with a stripy tail and large ears. Enquire within.' We couldn't put our address because of Mrs Renton, but Mrs Cousins knows Mrs Renton and doesn't like her so she said she would take the name and address if anyone asked and then, every evening after school, I called at the shop. We had Byron's old cat-basket ready so that I could take Camouflage straight away to her real home; but nobody enquired within. The first two days I hoped very much that someone would claim Camouflage, although I didn't want to part with her. But after that I didn't think anyone would claim her, and I began to hope they wouldn't.

Next Mummy put a notice in the *Knaresley Gazette* which comes out on Fridays and it said the same thing as the other one, except that it finished 'Enquire The Corner Shop, Station Road.' Mrs Cousins very kindly let us put her address and said she would deal with any enquiries. Once more, at first I hoped someone would claim Camouflage and, when no one did, I began to hope no one would.

Meanwhile Camouflage lived with us. She came and went by way of the plum tree so she didn't have to pass through Mrs Renton's part of the house and once she was indoors we were very careful to see that she didn't wander about on the staircase. Even so it wasn't quite safe because Mrs Renton often comes and sticks her head into our room, knocking on the door but not waiting for anyone to answer it, which infuriates my mother. 'We pay her rent – why can't she allow us a little privacy?' she says, but not to Mrs Renton. 'I suppose she wants to see that her pictures are still up and that we haven't scratched her deplorable furniture.' She always finds some excuse, of course, for her visits, such as that we haven't cleaned the bath which we share with her, unfortunately, or that I've been using her loofah; which I wouldn't dream of doing. 'Who'd want to use that filthy thing of hers?' complains my mother. 'It's just an excuse to come and look inside our room.'

Mrs Renton did look in twice while Camouflage was there.

One time I was doing my homework sitting at the table with the cat on my lap under the table and consequently she was quite hidden; the other time she was lying stretched out on the hearth rug but fortunately she was true to her name, since the hearth rug is hairy and buff. Nevertheless Mrs Renton was getting suspicious. Camouflage had only been with us a week when she told my mother she couldn't have her Ruth encouraging stray cats, so she must have seen Camouflage about sometime. I wonder whether the bad cat tried to get into the house while we were out or came and hampered Mrs Renton while she was scrubbing the tiled path. Perhaps she saw her going up the plum tree. But she had no proof.

Camouflage is not like other cats. She has a mind of her own but she does like a bit of company, and she likes going for walks. In the morning when we left for school we would put her out on the balcony. She would sit on the window-sill indignantly asking to be let in again but as soon as she saw us coming out of the house she would be down the tree in a trice and go trotting along with us, beside us or in front of us, as often as not stopping at every other step and almost tripping us up. Sometimes she would find business of her own before we had gone very far, or if we met a dog she would make herself scarce; but sometimes she came all the way to school with me, and only when she saw all the other girls in the school play-ground, waiting to be let in, would she disappear. When I came home from school she would often meet me somewhere on the way, coming out of a garden or through the hole in some hedge where she had been keeping watch. I was always very anxious, though, about the traffic, as she had no road sense and would dash across in front of a car if she suddenly caught sight of me. I used to go very carefully, watching to see if she was sitting waiting for me anywhere when I came back from school, so that I could wait until the road was clear before attracting her attention.

Because she was so fond of walking with me I began to wonder if I could not take her out for a proper walk with me, like a dog. I often go out into the country on my own now we live in Knaresley. I go on my bicycle and sometimes I leave it somewhere and explore. The town stands just at the entrance to the dale and if you go out of the town beyond my school, as soon as you are through Hackfall Woods, the fells close in on either side and you are in a steep-sided valley which is only about two fields wide at the bottom. At school they told us that there were once glaciers in these parts, long, long ago in the ice age, and that this is the reason for the shape of the valleys which are scooped out like troughs. I used often to go up the dale as far as Grewelthwaite, which is about three miles, and leave my bicycle there. Next to the village is a waterfall. Bowden Beck is the name of the river there, and it comes down through a little wood above the village and then falls down into a deep cavern of rock arched over with trees. It is always dark and dank in there with no sound but the falling of water. From there there is a footpath and one can follow the beck upstream, but I never went very far because I don't really like cows, and if there were bullocks I was very nervous in those days because I was never sure they weren't bulls.

I used to go all alone and so as to have something to do I took my sketch book which I was given last Christmas and my paintbox and I made several pictures of the waterfall one of which is rather good, I think, though Mummy likes the one I did of some cottages on the green at Grewelthwaite better. But it was rather lonely all by myself. Mummy is always tell-ing me that I *ought* to make some friends at school, but she

25

doesn't realise how difficult it is. It is a small private school and when I arrived everyone had their own friends already, as was natural when they'd all been at school together for years. I don't think it helps, either, that the classes are so small, though that's the reason Mummy sent me to this school instead of the Grammar School. At least, that's the reason she says, only I think it's actually because she lost her temper with the head-master of the Grammar School. She lost her temper with every-one at that time, just because she was so angry with Daddy for going away so that she couldn't lose her temper with him. Perhaps I wouldn't have made any friends at the Grammar School either. But as it is, at weekends, when I don't want to hang around at Mrs Renton's dreadful house, drawing Mummy's attention to the fact that I haven't yet made any friends, I go out into the country on my bicycle, all by myself. 'So you're off sketching,' says my mother. And then some-times she says, 'why don't you find someone to go with you?' So it occurred to me that Camouflage would be the very person to go with me.

I decided to try the experiment one Wednesday afternoon after Camouflage had been with us about a week. We have Wednesday afternoons off at our school, and Mummy doesn't, so she wouldn't be able to tell me it was a stupid idea and raise all sorts of objections. I put Camouflage in Byron's basket and strapped it on to my carrier with a rubber strap I have. At first she kept moving about inside which made the bicycle awfully wobbly, but I rode very carefully and presently she settled down. I had intended to go up to the waterfall but just before the village there is a little hump-backed bridge which crosses the river and the signboard pointing across it says 'No Road for Motors'. I had not been over it before, but seeing that I wanted to find a place without any traffic for Camouflage, it looked very tempting. So I changed my plans, and we turned across the bridge. We would be avoiding the cows.

No Road for Motors, after it had crossed the beck, went a little way upstream beside it and then turned towards the far side of the dale. It passed a large house, and then went on between walls. It was a perfectly good asphalted road and I still rode on my bicycle. I decided to see where it went before I let Camouflage loose. We crossed a bridge over a tiny stream beside which, amongst some trees, stood a little house. As soon as it passed the house the road petered out into a track. I leant my bicycle against a wall and took off the basket, unfastened it and opened the lid. Camouflage sat up inside and looked around, her nose twitching. She uttered several questioning miaows and then jumped out and began a systematic investigation of the situation. I sat down on the grass by the roadside and followed her with my eyes. I wondered what she would do. Every now and then she paused in her investigation, tossed her head at me and miaowed.

Presently she found the gate of the house and decided that it must be opened for her. 'No, puss,' I said, 'that's somebody's house,' and then I began to wonder if it was because the garden was so overgrown. Over the wall one could see a quantity of nettles, cabbages which had bolted and the great round pompoms of onion flowers. Then I saw, almost hidden by a bush, a notice which said 'For Sale'.

'Let's have a look,' I said to Camouflage. She was delighted when I opened the gate and she ran up the garden path and miaowed at the front door, which was, of course, locked. The windows of the house were all shuttered and we could not look in, so we returned to the road and went round the back. One end of the building was not house at all, but a cowhouse which was two storeys high. The kitchen stuck out at the back and not only was the window unshuttered, but I found that with a little manœuvring with a piece of wire that came from the cowhouse I could lift the catch. Camouflage went in first and I followed.

The kitchen had a flagged floor, a large sink, a kitchen range, and numerous cupboards with their doors standing open. The shelf paper was faded and dirty and the only sign of recent occupation was an empty Vim tin on the draining board.

On the ground floor were two other rooms with the front door and staircase in between them. The sunlight came through the cracks in the shutters and when my eyes got used to the darkness I could see quite well. The rooms were quite empty but on the flowery wallpaper I could see the unfaded patches where furniture had stood and pictures had hung. Upstairs were three more rooms, but there was no bathroom or lavatory in the place and only one tap in the kitchen.

Camouflage and I enjoyed ourselves exploring the whole house and then we climbed out of the window again. A path led from the back door to the stream and it was there that I discovered a most convenient privy. The stream had been diverted to run under a little stone-built hut, inside which was a proper wooden seat, and through the hole I could see the brown water rushing and swirling. There was even lavatory paper provided, the second sign of recent occupation.

All the time we were going round the house I was day-dreaming. It was out of the question, I know. It was for sale, anyway, not to let, and no bathroom. Probably damp too, I thought, sniffing the smell houses get when they are unoccupied. And even if it had been perfect in every respect, Mummy would have raised objections. She always does, auto-matically, to anything one suggests. Daddy was always sug-gesting we should move out of 'that barrack' since she disliked it so much, but she wouldn't hear of any of his suggestions.

It would be so nice if we didn't have to live at Mrs Renton's, but had some place where we could keep Camouflage...

However, I put it out of my mind.

The fell rose so steeply beyond the house that it almost seemed to stick out of the hillside. There was a stile over the wall made by extra-long stones which stuck out on either side for steps, and Camouflage and I went over it and clambered up the field beyond because I wanted to look down on the house from above and see if one could really drop pebbles down the chimney like the house in Beatrix Potter; one almost could have done, given a very good aim. Through the wall at the top of the field was a gap or chink, made not wide enough for cows to go through but splendid for cats and people. And on the other side was No Road for Motors, which had taken a loop and was going steeply up the hill. It really was No Road for Motors now, just stones and bare rock.

I went on up and up, puffing and panting, with Camouflage trotting along behind or in front, miaowing continually to say 'Don't leave me behind' or 'Hurry up, why must you lag so?' At first there were some trees and bushes in sight, but presently we got over the shoulder of the fell and it was much barer, with nothing but dry-stone walls running here and there. The road itself was now just a grassy track running along between two walls. I was glad of the walls because there were some fierce-looking cattle ranging about on the fells, and one, I am sure, was a bull.

The cottage was lost from view now, and so was Grewelthwaite and the whole of the dale. The fell goes up in sharp steps and we were over the edge of the first one so that all I could see was sky and the higher fells rising ahead. I might have been the only person alive on earth, and I would have been frightened to go on if I had been alone, but with Camouflage I felt quite brave. The only sound was the wind and the lonesome and forlorn cry of a far off bird which I found out later is called a curlew. Actually I enjoyed walking all alone there with Camouflage. It was far less lonely than being all by myself on the school playground with all the other girls milling round and none of them talking to me, or going in a crocodile when everyone else has a partner and I am walking at the back, either by myself or with someone else who has been left over too and doesn't want to walk with me anyway.

No Road for Motors did not go any higher up the fell but went on along the level. I was very curious to see where it led to eventually so we walked on, Camouflage and I, and after quite a long time we came to the edge once more, where we could look down into the valley. Grewelthwaite could no longer be seen; it was round a corner of the valley. The beck was hidden by trees from where we looked but we could see the road below us that goes on up the dale from Grewelthwaite to Kettleside and then goes over the top into Wensleydale.

No Road for Motors began to descend steeply and really I should have turned back because although I have no watch I could guess that time was getting on and of course Mummy gets worried if I am out too long. However, we went down the hill, which we did at a run and Camouflage got very excited, racing ahead of me and hiding and pouncing out, careering sideways across the road so that it was very difficult to avoid falling over her especially as I was coming down very fast. When we got down on to the flat I was still running like something on wheels that can't stop, until I almost tripped and threw myself on the grass and rolled there while Camouflage darted to and fro and pretended she didn't dare come right up to me and that I was trying to catch her.

When I stood up I found we were on a smooth piece of turf which sloped gently down to the river. The river was running rather quietly, not gurgling and rushing as it does below Grewelthwaite, and at this point it spread itself out very wide and shallow and No Road for Motors went right through it in a ford. I could see the cart tracks on the river bed and they came out on the other side and went up the bank to join the metalled road. Just below the ford the river was crossed by stepping-stones. I love crossing rivers by stepping-stones. I did not know what Camouflage would think of them. Perhaps I would have to come back and carry her across. Anyway I started out by myself, stepping from stone to stone.

Camouflage stayed on the shore, mewing piteously. She put a paw gingerly in the water and drew it back hurriedly in disgust, and mewed indignantly to me. I stopped in midstream. 'Come on, puss,' I called. 'Jump!'

It was not far from stone to stone, but she did not like the water. I started to come back. But when I reached her on the shore she ran away and would not let me catch her.

I went out a few stones. She came to the edge of the bank. I stepped a stone nearer. She fled away. I went out into the middle of the river again. She ventured back to the shore. She stretched out a paw towards the first stone which she could not reach without jumping. Then she decided to be brave. But having reached the first stone she started mewing helplessly once more. I did not budge. At last she came, bounding from stone to stone without any difficulty. She passed my stone and went one beyond. There she stopped and turned round, challenging me to come on, but how could I, when she was occupying the very place on to which I had to step?

I thought we were never going to get across, and I wanted to go back by the metalled road, in case it was quicker. I knew it

31

was getting late, almost tea time already. I managed to insert a foot on Pussy's stone but as soon as I was standing there she was occupying the next one and it was the same difficulty all over again.

Then we came to a place where one of the stones had fallen over and was almost under water, only one slippery wet piece jutting out. When I arrived on the stone before it, Camouflage stayed put, rubbing herself up against my legs and mewing. She wasn't going to jump on to that stone. I picked her up. It was very difficult to balance with her struggling in my arms but I held on tightly and put my foot on to the wet stone. I felt about until I had got it firmly placed and then took my other foot off the safe stone. Camouflage gave a gigantic squirm and jumped out of my arms on to the dry stone ahead of us. I sat down in the water.

It was at this moment I realised that we were being watched.

4

Michael

On the far shore, by the very edge, grew a great sycamore tree whose lower branches stretched right out over the water. The leaves almost hid a boy who was sitting astride a branch dangling his legs over the river. He was grinning. I pretended not to notice him.

Since I was already wet I did not bother to climb back on to the stepping-stones but waded through the ford on to the shore. At first Camouflage was rather taken aback at being deserted on her stone, but presently she decided to complete her crossing instead of sitting mewing where she was as if she was quite helpless. Still ignoring the boy, I tried to wring some of the water out of my skirt.

Suddenly he spoke. 'You looked fair daft,' he said. 'What did you do that for?'

Aren't people silly, the way they say 'what did you do that for?' when you drop something or fall over by accident? I was very cross anyway, so I said, 'Because I wanted to.'

He was silent. I took off my shoes and emptied the water out of them, took off my socks, and then wondered if I would put my shoes on again or go barefoot.

'You're sopping wet,' he said.

'Of course.'

When he had first spoken, Camouflage had looked round distractedly to see where the voice came from but had not been able to see him because of the leaves. But when he spoke again she caught sight of him and immediately she ran up the tree. She ran out on a branch above him and leaning down over his head she began to bat at him with her paw. As soon as he put out his hand to catch her she jumped on to a higher branch and continued to make lightning attacks on him from above. It was not at all easy for him to defend himself without over-balancing. I was much amused. I only hoped he would not knock Camouflage off into the river. But actually he seemed to be frightened of doing this himself, which made me think that he wasn't so bad after all.

'Is this your cat?' he asked.

'No,' I replied.

'She's a devil,' he said, ducking.

He managed to stand up, which made Camouflage flee to the top of the tree, so that he was able to edge his way to the trunk without hindrance, and he swung himself to the ground. We looked each other up and down.

'Well,' he said, 'you'd better come home with me and dry your things round the kitchen stove.'

As soon as I saw him properly an awful thought struck me. He was in Grammar School uniform. His bicycle and satchel lay on the grass beside the road. He was obviously on his way back from school. That meant that my mother would also be on her way back from school. And she would start wondering where I was. And here was I, probably miles from my bicycle, soaking wet and with Camouflage to get home too, and she might be tired by now. I felt hopeless and miserable, and though he now seemed a much nicer and kinder boy than I had thought at first I could only say, 'I'm sorry, I can't. My mother won't know where I've got to.'

'You can always give her a ring,' he said.

I had never thought of that. 'Oh, I say, have you got a telephone?' I asked eagerly. 'I'd be terribly grateful if I could use it.'

'Come on then,' he said. 'Will the cat come and all?'

At that moment Camouflage came running down the tree and as we went along I explained to him how she wasn't my cat and about the wicked Mrs Renton and so on. I also found out about him that his name was Michael Metcalfe and he was the same age as me, twelve. The farm where he lived, which was called Bowden Farm, was about a couple of hundred yards from the ford, standing well sheltered by trees a little back from the river.

Michael and I went into the kitchen but Camouflage refused to enter the house. The door was left ajar for her but she would only sit outside mewing piteously and if anyone tried to fetch her in she ran away as fast as she could go. Mrs Metcalfe tried to coax her in with a saucer of milk which she left just inside the door.

'Now just leave her be. She'll come in when it suits her,' she said. Meanwhile I had stripped off my wet clothes, been wrapped up in a blanket and my shoes had been stuffed with paper and my clothes hung on a line above the Aga. Mrs

35

Metcalfe rang up my mother and explained to her what had happened. But still Camouflage would not come in. She appeared on the window-sill, mewing very loudly and unhappily, but as soon as the window was opened she ran away.

Tea was laid in the kitchen. I had been invited to stay to tea while my things dried. Just as we had sat down Camouflage reappeared at the window. This time we managed it rather better. I stood and talked to her through the window while Michael went outside and caught her from behind and carried her struggling indoors.

All the time we were eating tea she ranged about the room on tiptoe as if it was enemy territory. In the excitement earlier I had not noticed, fast asleep in a box by the Aga, a huge tabby cat. At some point he had wakened and now, his head raised, he followed every movement of Camouflage with his eyes. She had not noticed him and she came right up to the box where he was, so that her face was only about a foot from his, when he gave a soft little hiss. For a full minute they gazed at one another without twitching a hair and then Camouflage gingerly backed away and continued her exploration while still watching the other cat out of the corner of her eye.

After tea she became more friendly, drank the milk that had been put for her and sat on Mrs Metcalfe's lap and afterwards on Michael's. Tigger, as the other cat was called, was disgusted by the attention she received in his own kitchen and jumped out of his box, stalked to the back door and demanded to be let out.

In the end Mr Metcalfe took me home in his jeep. We went up No Road for Motors to fetch my bicycle and the cat basket. He just dropped me at Mrs Renton's door and did not come in, of which I was quite glad because I had not explained to him about Mrs Renton and I was afraid we might meet her and he would say something about Camouflage, and so, quite literally, the cat would be out of the bag.

As I went upstairs I was planning how I would tell my mother all about it and I thought she would be pleased that I had made a friend, for I already regarded Michael as a friend because he was fond of cats and took a great interest in Camouflage and how we were to look after her and, when his mother said I must come again, said I must bring her too. But as soon as I got upstairs my mother began firing questions at me and she was obviously not in a good temper. She asked me how far I had been and where we had walked and she said I must never go up the fell by myself, just think, suppose I had twisted my ankle, it might have been days before anyone found me. And as for falling in the river, she didn't take any notice when I explained it was very shallow, a ford and quite safe, I couldn't have been drowned. She pretended to think that I would have been carried away by the current if Michael had not been there although I told her what had really happened. She made me promise that I would never go off into the wilds all by myself again, and went on and on, although, before, she had never stopped me going off on my bicycle to make sketches. You never can tell what grown-ups are going to get all het up about.

5

Now, isn't that
Miss Barnaby's cat?

It was the day after this, when I went into the corner shop on the way home from school to find out if there had been any answers to our advertisements, that Mrs Cousins told me the awful news. Mrs Renton herself had noticed the advertisements and had come in to ask Mrs Cousins who had put them in. Of course Mrs Cousins was very careful not to give us away, but Mrs Renton said, 'I suppose it's the same cat that is always hanging around my house. If nobody claims it, I shall have to have it put down.' She even said in a mysterious way that she 'had her suspicions' and talked about putting down poison if the cat did not make itself scarce, according to Mrs Cousins.

'You had better try to find a home for the poor pussy,' Mrs Cousins said to me. She said she would have taken her herself but she had a cat of her own who certainly would not allow it.

I went home full of despair and tried to think of some plan of action. There was no kind Mrs Raines in Knaresley, and anyway she had Byron already.

Camouflage appeared on the windowsill soon after I had come in and I wished I could warn her about the poison and explain to her that although we would love to keep her we couldn't, and she had better find another home. But what's the use of talking to cats? It's only in books for tiny tots that animals are able to speak or understand human language. When my mother came in I told her what I had heard, but she was in a bad mood and only exclaimed, 'Well, what do you expect me to do? Put down poison for Mrs Renton? You know we can't keep that cat, so don't be so ridiculous.' She is often like this on Thursdays because she teaches 4C all afternoon.

All the time I was doing my homework I was really trying to think what I could possibly do about Camouflage and in the end I worked out a plan, or rather two plans, so that if one didn't work I could use the other.

One plan was to ask Michael's mother if she could take the cat, which she probably couldn't because of Tigger, or could find someone else who would. My trouble was that I didn't know lots of people to ask who might want a cat, but Mrs Metcalfe must have lots of friends and besides, as it was some way out of Knaresley, Camouflage would not find her way back to us, or so I thought.

My second plan was to keep her at Fell Cottage (which was

the name of the little house along No Road for Motors) and to go out every day to visit her and feed her. Perhaps Michael would help me with this. I did not know where I would get the food from if my mother did not approve of the plan. Perhaps I could smuggle out some school dinner in a polythene bag.

Anyway, what I decided to do was to take Camouflage to Fell Cottage straight away, so as to get her out of danger, and then to ask Michael and his mother for help. I would have to get up specially early the next morning so that I could take my bicycle and go up to Fell Cottage before school. I did not tell my mother so that she would not have a chance to forbid me. Not that going as far as Fell Cottage by myself was the same thing as going up on to the fells by myself, which I wasn't allowed to do; but you never know what things grown-ups are going to disapprove of, and going up to Grewelthwaite before school and leaving a cat in a deserted cottage might be one of them.

But I never thought my mother would be so angry at my getting up early and getting the breakfast. I was just coming upstairs with the milk and the post when she burst out of her room, not yet dressed.

'What on earth are you doing, creeping about the house at this hour of night?' she exclaimed.

'It's not night,' I said. 'It's morning.'

'Give me those letters,' she said and snatched them from me before I had time to hand them to her. Then she looked at her watch. 'Ten past seven! Since when have you been getting up at ten past seven? I could have had another twenty minutes in bed.' (She hates getting up in the morning.) 'And you're dressed already. Whatever possessed you to get up at this unearthly hour?'

'I was just getting the breakfast. I thought it might help,' I said in an injured voice, feeling rather guilty because I knew that wasn't why I'd done it.

She snorted and went back into her room. Later she reappeared dressed and smiling. 'How sweet of you to get the breakfast, darling,' she said. 'I'm sorry I was angry just now. I thought it was much earlier than it was. It was a very kind thought. Only really I'd rather you didn't go wandering downstairs before I'm up. You know what Mrs Renton's like.'

'I only went to get the milk.'

'I know, only promise me you won't do it again. I mean, I'd love it if you got the breakfast, only wait until I'm up before you go downstairs. Promise?'

'All right,' I said, and added rather grumpily, 'I wasn't doing anything she could object to.'

'She might not like it if she found you going through the letters to see which were for us,' said my mother. 'She'd find fault with anything. I think it's better if I'm always the first to go down and fetch the post. Understand?'

Well, I didn't understand. I couldn't think why she made such a fuss. It puzzled me. But anyway she was touched I had got the breakfast, and she was sorry she had snapped at me, so I got away early without any difficulty and managed to smuggle Camouflage out with me.

I popped Camouflage in at the kitchen window of Fell Cottage and shut it after her. If she was to live there I did not want to have to shut her in all the time, but she would have to get used to it first. I gave her some food before I left her to distract her attention. Then I planned to come back after school to give her another meal, and if possible bring Michael with me.

As soon as our school was over I went down to the Grammar School gates in the hope of catching Michael as he came out. The Grammar School finishes ten minutes after ours so I had a fair chance of not missing him. All the children started pouring out and I waited and waited and still Michael did not come. I began to wish I had never thought of this idea and almost decided to go away without waiting any longer, although there were still a few children coming out. I was afraid he would come out with some other boys and then he would be ashamed of finding a girl waiting for him. Perhaps it would be better to ride up to Bowden Farm.

However, at this moment he appeared, by himself, carrying a violin. 'Hullo, what are you doing here?' he said.

'I was waiting to speak to you.'

'I had a music lesson,' he explained. 'What do you want?'

I explained about Camouflage. Meanwhile he fastened his violin on to his bicycle, and we started off together towards Grewelthwaite.

'Of course, we'll look after her,' he said. 'Me Mum's very fond of cats.'

'What about Tigger?' I asked.

'Tigger'll have to lump it. We used to have two cats before, until our Marmaduke died. They never spoke when they met.'

I was so relieved. It seemed all my troubles were over. We turned up No Road for Motors and arrived at Fell Cottage. I opened the kitchen window and called Camouflage. She did not come.

At first I thought she was just sulking because I had left her shut up all day long. We climbed into the house, taking care to shut the kitchen window behind us, and hunted everywhere, calling all the time. At last we decided that she could be nowhere in the house, though how she could have got out we could not tell. We searched the cowhouse and the privy, we unpiled a great pile of firewood because I thought I could see her eyes gleaming in the darkness in the middle of it, but she was not there. We called and called. It was getting late. I knew my mother would be worrying.

'I know what,' said Michael, 'she got out and then, of course, she went along No Road for Motors, the way she's been before. I reckon she's at our house by now.'

We decided that I would go home and he would go home and if Camouflage should turn up at Bowden Farm he would ring me up to let me know. If not, we would meet the next morning, Saturday, at Fell Cottage, and make a second search. I told him how my mother would not let me go out on the fell alone, but if there were two of us it would be all right, so we fixed to bring sandwiches and search all the way along No Road for Motors. Meanwhile I left a plate of food outside the kitchen door at Fell Cottage.

When we rode up to Fell Cottage I thought all my troubles were over. When we rode away I was despairing once more and I only tried to put a brave face on it so as not to seem ungrateful to Michael who was very kind and helpful.

I rode home, put my bicycle away, and went round to the front door. I thought I heard a mew, but I told myself it was just imagination. I was very miserable. Dr Bradwell, who is our doctor, was walking down the street. He smiled and said, 'Hullo.' I was just hunting for my key when he stopped and exclaimed:

'Now, isn't that Miss Barnaby's cat?'

6

I meet a very eccentric
old lady

There was Camouflage sitting up the plum tree.

'Who's Miss Barnaby?' I asked. 'We can't find out whose cat it is.'

Miss Barnaby, he told me, was an old lady who lived in Palace Road. The reason why Camouflage was so different from other cats in her markings and everything was because she was an Abyssinian cat. 'So far as I know Miss Barnaby is the only person in Knaresley who has a cat like that,' said the doctor, 'but I didn't know she had lost it.'

'Perhaps we could ring her up and ask her,' I suggested, because Palace Road is quite a way away.

'I'm afraid she hasn't got a telephone,' he said. 'You will find she is rather eccentric and doesn't go in for anything modern like that.'

I ran up to tell my mother.

'The sooner we get rid of that cat the better,' she said, 'or we'll have another row with Mrs Renton. You'd better take her round before it gets dark. I'm just getting the tea, so hurry.'

Despite what Mummy said it was already getting dark by the time I reached Palace Road. Palace Road is called that because the Bishop of Knaresley's Palace is on it. It is one of the main roads out of Knaresley and it is lit by those orange lights which make people look like corpses. They started to come on just as I was riding down it and immediately the evening seemed to turn into night. The houses in Palace Road are very large and stand separately among trees some way back from the road. None of them have numbers up, so it was completely dark before I found the right place.

The house was down a drive which led between dark evergreen trees, and it could not be seen from the road at all. I walked my bicycle down the drive, and was very glad I had bicycle lamps. The house was completely dark and deserted. There was not a chink of light anywhere. I suddenly began to feel frightened and wanted to go away immediately, but I told myself it was stupid. I unstrapped the cat basket from the bicycle, and I had to take the front lamp because I could not find the bell without it. It was one of those bells which are usually out of order, where you pull a handle in a socket. I pulled with all my might feeling sure nothing would happen; but I did hear a bell clanging somewhere a very long way off inside the house. After I had waited for some time I decided to ring again, count to 200, and then go. I had switched off the lamp so as not to waste the battery. I think I would have been more frightened if Camouflage had not been there inside the basket. She started to mew.

I had just reached 170 when the door opened. No lights had

gone on inside the house. There had been no sound of footsteps. A tiny little old lady stood there in the darkness holding a pocket torch in her hand. Her face and wispy white hair looked weird in the distant glow from the street lights. She blinked at me nervously.

'Are you Miss Barnaby?' I asked.

'Yes, dear. Now what is it you want? You gave me such a fright.'

'Please, Dr Bradwell told me this was your cat.'

'My what, dear?'

I wondered if she was deaf, but before I could repeat myself louder, Camouflage had made herself heard with the most strident mewings.

'Oh, you've brought back Pamela, have you? How very kind of you! Do come inside.'

She led me into the pitchy darkness of the hall. By the light of her minute torch she could just see her way and I followed her blindly. She opened a door and ushered me into a dark room. I bumped against some furniture.

'Oh dear!' she exclaimed, 'I've forgotten the matches,' and disappeared, torch and all, leaving me in utter darkness. Wherever I tried to move there seemed to be huge and unknown pieces of furniture. As my eyes got used to the darkness I could make out a light patch which was the window, but that was all. Camouflage was mewing again so I put the basket down on the floor and began to undo the straps.

At last Miss Barnaby came back with her torch and the matches. I wondered what she was going to light with them. It turned out to be gas. She lowered the lamp, which hung on a pulley from the ceiling, and in a moment the flame was lit and the room was so dazzlingly bright that I had to cover my eyes.

'That's better,' she said. 'Now is this really Pamela you've found? Why, so it is! You naughty puss! Where have you been all this time? Yes, you shall have some milk. Do sit down,' she added to me. 'I'll just get some milk,' and she scuttled out of the room once more.

Pamela or Camouflage (and if you say them you will see that they might sound rather the same to a cat's ear) was left with me. She did not examine the room. She was quite evidently at home. It was I instead who went round like a cat on tiptoe, peeping at everything.

In the middle of the room stood a huge mahogany table surrounded by eight chairs. A heavy mahogany sideboard stood at one side of the room. Over it, in a gilt frame, was a picture of long-haired cattle in a mist. I wondered what my mother would think of it. The mantelpiece was very elaborate. It went right up to the ceiling with a mirror in the middle and little shelves and niches on either side and on each little shelf was an ornament under a glass dome and in the middle was a gold clock with all its works showing, also under a dome. To one side of the fireplace stood a cabinet with glass doors and inside some china was arranged, obviously special china. There was a lot more furniture in the room, but these are the pieces I remember. I was just looking at a big picture which had its title under it, *The Stag at Bay*, by Landseer, when Miss Barnaby reappeared.

'That is rather a fine engraving, isn't it?' she said.

I didn't know what an engraving was, so I said, 'We've got a picture by him on the stairs called *The Old Shepherd's Chief Mourner*. My mother says it's sentimental.'

I wondered if I had said something rude but she only said, 'Your mother sounds a very sensible woman.'

She was carrying a bottle of milk in her hand, and Camouflage was clamouring to be given some.

'Oh, a saucer,' she said in dismay.

I thought she was going to have to make a third journey but instead she went over to the cabinet and took out one of the beautiful saucers, all blue and white and gold.

'Pamela is a very important person. She always expects the best Rockingham tea service.'

I was not quite sure whether she was serious or not. She kept a completely straight face.

'I'm afraid we only gave her very ordinary saucers,' I said.

'Now, you haven't told me who you are or where you come from – that is, where Pamela got to, and whom I have to thank for so kindly looking after her. Do sit down.'

'I really can't stay,' I said, remembering that my mother had told me to come back quickly. 'My mother will be wondering where I've got to. We live in Station Road.'

'Station Road? You mean Pamela has been right over the other side of Knaresley? And you have all that way to walk back on this dark night.'

'I've got my bicycle. But my mother might get cross, you know. I think I ought to go back now.'

She did not press me to sit down any longer. 'Of course you must go. I quite understand. Grown-ups can be very difficult.'

'The trouble is that you never know when they are going to be cross, and when they're not.'

'Ah yes, their behaviour is arbitrary and irrational.'

Suddenly I wondered once more if she was serious. After all, she was a grown-up herself. But she went on, 'I've had a lot of trouble with them myself. But one must make allowances. Things are much harder for them than one imagines. They have a hard life.'

'I think children have a hard life too,' I said. I could not make

48

out whether she was laughing at me or ticking me off in some obscure way.

'Do you?' she asked. And this time she did smile, in fact, I almost think she winked at me. 'Now, before you go, you must tell me your name and address. Perhaps I should write and thank your mother for her hospitality to Pamela.'

When I told her our address I explained that we had an awful landlady and how she had tried to poison Camouflage, as we had called Pamela.

'Isn't that Marion Renton's house?' she asked sharply.

'Oh, I'm sorry, I mean, if she's a friend of yours, I shouldn't have said all those things about her,' I exclaimed in dismay.

'I know Marion Renton of old, since she was not much older than you, with a pair of long thick plaits and a pudding face, but I would never have called her a friend of mine.'

'Oh, good,' I said, 'because I'm afraid I hate her.'

'One must make allowances even for her.'

'Has she had a hard life?'

'She has not had much joy of it, and if that is largely because she is incapable of joy, yet who are we to say that is her own fault? But I find it hard to make allowances for people without imagination. So often they destroy other people.'

After this, and many thanks, I left.

7

All the best people are mad

I rang up Michael to tell him about Camouflage. It was Mrs
Metcalfe who answered and she said, 'You must come over
anyway. Michael is counting on your coming.' I also went
into the corner shop (it stays open late) to tell Mrs Cousins.

'Miss Barnaby?' she said. 'Was it Miss Barnaby's cat?'

'Do you know Miss Barnaby?' I asked.

'Everyone knows of Miss Barnaby. Not that anyone sees
much of her nowadays. She is such a reclusive person. Does she
still live in that great house in Palace Road, all by herself? Oh,
they say she was a wild one in her young days. That was before
my time. She had marvellous red-gold hair and a will of her
own. She used to give music lessons when I was a girl. Mr
Renton, now, he was a pupil of hers. They say he was a marvellous player, 'cello I think it was, but he gave it all up when
he married. Mrs Renton wouldn't stand for it. She let him play

the piano, and the organ at the Methodist Chapel, but that was all.'

I wondered if that was what Miss Barnaby meant about Mrs Renton destroying people. Perhaps he wasted away and died because he wasn't allowed to play his 'cello.

My mother wasn't the least bit interested in Miss Barnaby. I tried to tell her about the house and how it was lit by gas but all she said was, 'Really? Well, I hope her cat doesn't come round here again.'

'What does reclusive mean?' I asked.

'Reclusive? I've never heard such a word. You mean recluse.'

'Well, what does it mean then? I'm sure Mrs Cousins said reclusive.'

'Then she meant recluse. It's a person who lives shut away from the world like a hermit.'

Michael was much more interested in Miss Barnaby when I told him about her next day. I told him how the house was all dark, so that I thought there could be nobody there and then suddenly the door opened and there she was with her pocket torch in her hand.

'But why didn't you hear her coming?'

'She was wearing some old tennis shoes.'

'What did she look like?'

'She was small and bent and her hair was white and wispy, though Mrs Cousins says it was red-gold when she was young. And she peered at me as if she hadn't got her glasses on and I was never quite sure if she meant just what she said. And once she almost winked at me. I think she's rather fun.' And I told him everything that had happened and how Mrs Cousins said she was very reclusive and nobody saw anything of her, though long ago she used to give music lessons. Michael asked me lots of questions and when he heard about the music lessons, he said, 'What did she teach? Piano?'

'I expect so,' I said and then I remembered and added, 'Actually I think Mrs Cousins said it was 'cello.'

'Ah,' said Michael, and after a pause he said, 'I wish I'd been there.' Later on he said, 'Do you think your Miss Barnaby would let you bring Camouflage out for a walk? She was such a funny cat.'

'I don't know,' I said. I didn't imagine I would ever ever see Miss Barnaby again. But later I began to wonder if Michael's idea were not a good one. I should like to see Camouflage again. Would I dare go round and visit Miss Barnaby, though? What excuse could I think of for going? And would it sound quite preposterous to a grown-up to suggest taking her cat out for the afternoon? Yet I had the feeling that Miss Barnaby was no ordinary grown-up, that she might be willing to join forces with children against the grown-up world. In fact, the more I thought of the possibility of taking Camouflage out the more I wanted to know more of Miss Barnaby. But I never got round to doing anything about it.

Then much to my surprise my mother got a letter which included a note for me. It was one of those printed invitation cards and it said:

Miss Pamela Camouflage
requests the pleasure of the company of
Miss Ruth Wintersgill to tea on Sunday at 4 o'clock

R.S.V.P.   *Miss Barnaby, 14, Palace Road,*
Knaresley.

'She says she hopes I won't mind her asking you,' my mother said. 'Do you want to go?'

Now, it was most odd my mother saying that. She always makes me accept invitations, whether I like it or not. I mean, invitations to parties from daughters of her friends, and then I have to ask them back to my parties and I don't suppose they want to come to my parties either, and so it goes on forever. But then she always wants me to be friends with the daughters of her friends which seems unreasonable to me because she never makes friends with the mothers of my friends. And we never hit it off, the daughters of her friends and I.

But the invitation from Miss Barnaby was apparently quite different. I didn't have to accept it. 'You don't have to go, you know,' she said. 'We can make up some excuse.' She had been talking to Mrs Cousins and she seemed to have picked up the idea that Miss Barnaby was quite mad. And anyway she wanted me to have friends of my own age. It never occurred to her that I could have a friend of Miss Barnaby's age.

'But I want to go,' I said.

She thought it was because I wanted to see Camouflage, and of course it was, partly. I let her think so because I could never have explained to her, indeed I would never have dreamt of telling her how Miss Barnaby had said that grown-ups are difficult.

So I went to tea there on Sunday. My mother had given me a long lecture on how I was to behave because she thinks I am a little hooligan with no manners and she thought Miss Barnaby would be a correct old lady who expected little girls to be seen and not heard. 'Put on a little of that old-world charm. I think you can when you try,' she said. 'Offer to go and fetch things, ask if you can help with the washing up and so on. I think you know what I mean.' I promised to do my best.

The house in Palace Road looked very different by daylight. To begin with, the garden, which one did not notice by dark, was an absolute jungle. There were lots of weeds in the gravel patch outside the front door, giant sow thistles and tufts of grass. But where the real garden had been was quite impenetrable. A pergola had collapsed beneath a weight of roses whose huge shoots waved wildly in the air and became entangled in some lilac bushes. Over a thicket of greenery rose tall towers of seed vessels, some belonging to flowers like lupins and delphiniums, others to weeds like willow-herb.

Miss Barnaby caught me looking at this wilderness. 'The garden is getting on top of me,' she said. 'I went away for a month in the summer and I have never caught up.' Actually I don't think a thing had been done in the garden that summer, nor, probably, the summer before. But Miss Barnaby was very vague and I don't think she really noticed the state things were in. She said about the house, 'I can't afford to keep things up as they should be,' but again I don't think she noticed how ancient and dilapidated it all looked. The paintwork, which was of the brown, varnishy sort, was everywhere standing up in little islands the way paint goes when it is very ancient. The ceilings were practically black. The wallpapers were also brown. One never knows with those sorts of papers whether they were originally brown or just brown with age. I could still dimly see patterns of roses and trellis-work, the same sort of patterns that are favoured by Mrs Renton and that my mother can't abide; but Mummy would have liked the furniture, because Miss Barnaby has some really nice things. In the room she took me into was a piece that she told me was a square piano, all inlaid with different woods with a design of flowers, and very elegant legs. She showed me the bureau too, and a cabinet, because I showed an interest. 'They are my own things,' she said. 'All the heavy Victorian stuff belonged to my parents.'

She had taken me into a room at the back of the house which

looked much more lived in than the room I had been into before. Camouflage was sitting before the fire and looked up and greeted me when I came in. 'I trust she has not been over to see you again,' said Miss Barnaby, 'Though I daresay she finds life rather dull with no other company than me.'

When I say 'lived in' it is really an understatement. The room was a mess. Those lovely pieces of furniture were standing in the midst of the most incredible clutter. Every surface was covered with things, some of them ornaments, framed photographs and little framed texts supposed to look like samplers, and some of it just things that had been left there – cups and saucers, opened letters, books, cotton reels, scissors. There were still some of last year's Christmas cards on the mantelpiece. It looked as if she had never cleared anything away or dusted since she last did something in the garden. A faint odour (of cat? sour milk?) hung over the room. The upholstery was very old and worn and had been patched here and there with material that did not match, sewn with large stitches. I noticed one chair that should have had a cane seat, but it had gone through and a piece of oil-cloth had been tacked over to cover the damage. The windows were almost entirely grown over with creeper, so that I felt as if I were under water.

The table had been laid for tea with the same beautiful china in blue and white and gold that had been in the cabinet in the other room.

'The Rockingham tea-set,' I said.

'Yes,' said Miss Barnaby approvingly. 'I believe in using pretty things if one has them. I am growing old now, and who will enjoy them when I am dead? I shan't always be able to live in my own house with all my own things around me and nobody to look after me. One day, when I can no longer totter out to the kitchen by myself, they will pack me off to an institution where I shall sit at a long table with all the other old dears and eat off thick white crockery. So let us enjoy the good things while we are still able.'

This sounded very sad and I did not know what to say so I said something which I thought afterwards must have sounded very impertinent. I asked her, 'Do you see nobody at all?'

She rounded on me sharply. 'People have been telling you things.'

'They said you were a recluse.' I felt sure I had been rude.

'I assure you, Ruth – ' she said, 'I've got your name right haven't I? – let me assure you that I am quite mad really, and if anyone tells you the contrary, don't you believe them.'

I looked at her in astonishment but she had a wicked smile on her face so I smiled with relief.

'All the best people are mad,' she said. 'Have you discovered that yet? Only people like our friend Mrs Renton are sane. People say "mad" as if it were an insult, but really we should accept it as an honour. Unless, of course, you want to be one of the Mrs Rentons of this world.'

We went to the kitchen to make the tea and I was as helpful as I could be. The kitchen was even more 'lived in' – I mean, in an even greater mess. Considering the fuss some people make about hygiene I wonder that Miss Barnaby was still alive. I think it was largely that she never put things away. Perhaps when one is as old as that it requires too much energy to be always putting things in and out of cupboards, so that everything she used had accumulated on the draining board, the kitchen table, the dresser top. And amongst all this were things which had missed being washed up, scraps of food on plates and opened tins which were still half full. And a smell, of course, of food that was not quite right. Since every surface was covered there was nowhere to put anything down and she had to balance the beautiful Rockingham teapot on top of the gas stove and gave me the lid to hold while she made the tea. I was terrified there would be an accident, but all went well.

Since she had begun talking about Mrs Renton I asked her about Mr Renton and his playing the 'cello, and how Mrs Renton had made him give it up. 'Why did she do that?' I asked.

'She had no feeling for music herself. She used to come to me for piano lessons – I might as well have tried teaching her to fly! I suppose she wanted to reduce him to her own dimensions, to clip his wings because she had no wings herself.'

'But why did he let her?'

'He was a man who wanted someone to tell him what to do. Mrs Renton soon had him trained to wipe his shoes on the doormat and not to put his feet on the mantelpiece, and not to play that horrid 'cello which made her head ache so and was sure to disturb the neighbours. You see, he had talent, but no drive.'

'Couldn't you have driven him?' I asked. It seemed such a waste.

'I don't like to work other people like puppets,' she said, shaking her head. 'It's dangerous to try to influence people.'

'But if people like you refuse to influence people then they'll all fall under the influence of people like Mrs Renton. Don't you think that is a bad thing? I mean, why should the "sane" people always win?'

'Perhaps you're right,' she said, 'but being mad means that one thinks people should choose for themselves.'

After that we sat down to tea. I forget how I began to tell her all about myself. I think it started with Byron, and so on to leaving Horsepath and about my parents. I hadn't told anyone about it before. Really there had been no one to tell. I told her about how my mother had said that my father didn't want me, and how he hadn't sent me a birthday card or anything.

'Your poor mother!' she exclaimed. 'You shouldn't have told her you'd rather live with your father. Then she wouldn't have told you he didn't want you.'

'You mean it's a lie?' I asked.

'I know nothing about it. It could be.'

'You mean, I hurt her, so she wanted to hurt me back?'

I must have looked very shocked because she pulled a mock disapproving face and said, 'Very wicked, eh? Wouldn't you do the same?'

'But then . . .'

'But, what?'

'I thought grown-ups were supposed to behave better than children.' At that she only laughed.

'They're always telling us we'll know better when we're older.'

'One has to make a great many allowances for them,' she said.

'They have a hard life,' I chimed in.

'Exactly. But don't you believe a word I say,' she added. 'It's all the fault of that cat. It's years since I had anyone to tea. Camouflage insists on having her friends in and then I am tempted to influence them. And I only got a cat because I thought cats were decent self-sufficient animals who "walked by themselves"!'

'Camouflage is different from other cats,' I said, 'she likes walking with people. I took her for ever such a long walk over the fell from Grewelthwaite to Bowden Farm. My friend wondered if you would let us take her out again.'

'Camouflage,' she said, addressing the cat, 'have you another friend whom you haven't introduced to me? Someone else for me to influence?'

'His name is Michael Metcalfe and he lives at Bowden Farm,' I said.

'You must bring him to meet me. I can't have Camouflage going out with young men who have never been introduced to me.'

'I think he'd like to meet you,' I said. 'And then can we take her out? We were ever so careful with her. I took her in the basket until I got to a place called "No Road for Motors" because she is rather silly with traffic.'

'Yes, that was wise. You seem to have looked after her very well. But I must meet your friend first. Then, if I approve of him, you can take Camouflage out again.'

8

Another Miss Barnaby

It was a few days after this, when I had come home from school,
and Mummy found we had no butter, that she sent me down
to the corner shop. We had had our tea, but the corner shop
stays open late. There were several people in there, doing
their shopping after work, and I noticed a Grammar School
boy examining the sweets. I had been waiting in the queue
sometime before he turned round and I wasn't even looking so
it was he who recognised me.

'Hullo,' he said. 'It's you.'

'Michael,' I said in surprise. 'What are you doing here?'

'My Dad and Mum have gone over to Pudsey to see an aunt.
I was supposed to stay at school till they pick me up on the
way home, but I don't like being with the boarders so I slipped
away.'

'Come up to my place,' I said. 'I'm sure my Mum would like to meet you.'

I was still waiting for the butter so he waited too.

'Did you ask Miss Barnaby if we could take Camouflage out?' he asked me.

'Yes,' I said. 'She asked me to tea. I like her ever so much, because she's different from other grown-ups. And I asked her, and she said I must bring you to see her first.'

'Let's go now, then.'

'Now?'

'Then we could take Camouflage out on Saturday. Otherwise when could I go to see her? I go home after school, and it gets dark so early now, my mother won't let me go out. Why not now?'

'I'll have to tell my mother. She won't know where I am.'

I wondered what she would say to this project but my mother has one advantage: when she is buried in a detective story she never bothers to listen to what I ask her but just grunts, so that afterwards I can say 'You said I could'. When I came in with Michael and said 'This is Michael' she didn't look up and when I said, 'I thought you'd like to meet him,' she said, 'Yes, dear,' without raising her eyes. 'We're going to see Miss Barnaby,' I said and she grunted and read on, so we went.

I went fearlessly up the dark drive, even without a bicycle lamp which I hadn't brought, and I knew where to find the bell-pull. After quite a wait we heard the creak of a door within and the flip-flop of slippers across the floor. There was a faint glimmer of light through the fan-light. Miss Barnaby was carrying a candle. She held it below her face so that the light was cast upwards across her features giving her the look of a ghoulish mask.

'I hope you don't mind,' I said, 'I brought Michael to see you, as you said.'

'How do you do?' she said.

They shook hands.

'How do you do?'

'Come in,' she said.

She led the way with the candle into another large room I had not been into before. More candles stood on a grand piano in spreading candelabra, and a music stand stood close by to catch their light. High up, the light flickered on some white busts which stood on top of heavy glass-fronted bookcases, and in the many panes of the bookcases, which were crookedly set, hundreds of other reflected candles appeared, all winking and wavering in the draught from the hall.

'I was in the middle,' she said. 'Sit down while I finish.'

Three very large leather covered chairs with buttons in their backs and arms supported on little wooden balustrades stood facing the piano. Camouflage was sitting in the middle one with her paws folded in front of her; Michael and I sat down in the other two. Miss Barnaby lifted her 'cello and sat down before the music stand.

Before, I had thought of Miss Barnaby as being very old, eccentric, a little old lady in a little old town who had some strange ideas which I found wiser than most other adult ideas I had come across. I liked her, I found her interesting. I had never imagined she was important.

Now before me sat a different Miss Barnaby.

I am not very musical. Michael understands these things much better than I do. So you will have to take it from him that she is a really wonderful 'cellist. All I know is that she was transformed while she was playing. I quite forgot the old lady whom I had first met with the thin wisps of white hair, standing at the doorway in her old tennis shoes, holding a pocket torch. I imagined what she must have been like when she was young and wild with red-gold hair and then I forgot that too and only saw the music because at that moment she seemed to have become the music she was playing. And yet one had an impression of complete silence and stillness as if everything was holding its breath to listen, straining every nerve with attention. The darkness was festooned with a hundred candle flames (or reflected candle flames) burning steadily with an upward movement like pricked ears; and behind the brightness of the candle flames stood the dark shapes of the furniture like an unknown audience in the shadows, while the white busts (which I found out afterwards were the busts of great musicians) seemed, in the slight movement of the light, to be alive, intent, enthralled.

My legs were hanging over the edge of the leather chair and the back of the chair was two feet behind my back. My hands lay in my lap. Camouflage reclined towards the front of her chair, paws crossed, head raised, ears erect and her amber cat's eyes glinting in the dark. Michael's feet reached the floor and he sat elbow on knee, chin in hand. I watched him, but he never looked at me. His eyes never left her. He looked to me as if he was under a spell.

When at last she came to an end we still sat transfixed. It was Camouflage that moved first. With a 'Prrree-i-ooo-m' she rose to her feet and stretched.

'Camouflage always knows when I'm finished,' said Miss Barnaby.

'She never claps at the end of a movement,' said Michael.

This was mumbo jumbo to me but it seemed to please Miss

Barnaby. She asked Michael what instrument he played, who taught him and they talked music in a very professional manner.

'Well,' she said at last, 'I'm very pleased to have met you. I'm sure you will make an excellent friend for Camouflage.'

'We may take her out then?' asked Michael.

'Yes, if you look after her and keep her away from traffic.'

'On Saturday?'

'I can come and fetch her,' I said.

'When is she to be ready? She will want to wash her whiskers and preen her ears.'

'Can I come about ten?'

As we left, walking down the drive, Michael said in tones of awe, 'You never told me she was like that.'

Taking out Camouflage became a regular Saturday institution after that. I would call for her in the morning and take her out to No Road for Motors where Michael would meet me on his bicycle. We would walk over the shoulder of the fell and come down to the stepping-stones which Camouflage now knew so well that she would race ahead of us down to the water's edge and out across the stones. Half-way across she would stop and watch the water gurgling, racing, bubbling through the gap. When we caught up with her she would not budge but conduct a conversation with indignant mews. Sometimes she attempted fishing, dipping a paw in the rushing water. She never caught anything. Sometimes she would rush back to the shore she had come from and refuse to cross with us, but we learnt in time that she would turn up (indignant) at the farm a little later if we left her. There we had lunch as it was getting too late in the year to eat a picnic. Indeed these walks went on all through the winter months when the fell rang hard as iron under our feet and all the thistles and little plants were fretted with frost into the most intricate star-like jewellery. There was not much snow that winter except higher up the fell but one day there was a thin fall of snow all over the dale. It was like black edged notepaper for mourning, all the drystone walls dividing up the valley and the fells into white patches. Camouflage did not know what to make of the snow. She picked her feet up and shook them in between steps and mewed in a complaining way as if to say, 'What's all this for?' As No Road for Motors went up the fell the snow became deeper and had formed drifts in hollows and against walls. Camouflage, chasing a leaf, ran into a drift which came up to her whiskers. She looked at us as if we had done it on purpose and thereafter treated snow with very great suspicion. When the snow had blown a little thicker across the track she stopped dead and made a great clamour and in the end we had to carry her across the thick part.

The following weekend a little more snow had fallen and the crust had frozen so hard that when one trod on it it was a moment before it gave way beneath the feet. Camouflage being much lighter than we were could walk on the surface without going through at all. After a little preliminary caution, for fear this was all planned to take her in, she discovered she was quite safe and proceeded to cut the wildest capers.

Everything was so still up there. The silence was weird. The sky was a whitish grey and the earth was a greyish white and the only sound was when the wind disturbed some loose powdered frozen snow and sent it rattling across the crisp crust into another gulley to rest. I was glad Camouflage was so gay.

All the smaller rivulets were frozen and I hoped I'd see the big waterfall at Grewelthwaite all icicles as it is on a postcard you can buy at the post office, but then the thaw set in. We stopped going over No Road for Motors because the stepping-stones were under water. The river was in spate and the water-fall looked magnificent and made so much noise that we could still hear it, very dimly like distant thunder, at Fell Cottage. Everyone was congratulating themselves on the mildness of the winter, but I couldn't help wishing it had been more spectacular. Now there was nowhere we could walk because it was muddy everywhere. My mother bought me some Wellington boots and made me wear them all the time which is not very comfortable for walking and even worse for riding a bicycle. 'You're not going to catch a cold,' she said, 'because it's me that will suffer for it if you do. If you don't want to wear the boots you don't have to go out.'

After all the fuss my mother had made about my not having any little friends you would have thought she would have been pleased that I'd found Michael. But she seemed to think it was odd his being a boy and even odder that Miss Barnaby should take an interest in us when she was famous for taking an interest in nobody.

'I've found out all about Miss Barnaby,' she announced one day. I felt like saying, 'You don't know a thing that matters about her,' but instead I kept silent.

'Well, don't you want to hear?'

They had been discussing Miss Barnaby in the staff room. 'She was very emancipated in her youth. Her parents were very rich and she was the only child. They gave her everything she asked for and they allowed her to go up to London to study music, though everyone in Knaresley thought that was very daring in those days. And they thought when she was finished she would come home to grace the paternal hearth with her accomplishments but she scandalised the town by getting a job with a big orchestra. It's not as if she had to earn her living, everyone said. She was such a good looker, they say, that she had numbers of admirers but she turned down all their proposals. So of course people began to talk and they even said she was really in love with the conductor of this orchestra, who was a married man. I daresay it was all untrue but, when they heard the rumours, her mother and father begged her to come home, and she refused. Then came the war, the 1914–18 war, in which this conductor was killed, and soon afterwards old Pa Barnaby's dyeworks began to lose money heavily and all of a sudden they found they weren't as rich as they had been. And then Mrs Barnaby's health began to fail and at last her daughter came home to nurse her. Everyone says that she thought that it would only be for a short while until her mother died, but in fact Mrs Barnaby hung on for another five years and by the time she had passed away, Mr Barnaby needed nursing in his turn. To make ends meet, since they were rather poor by this time, Miss Barnaby gave music lessons.'

'I know that,' I said, 'I told you she taught Mrs Renton and Mr Renton, too.'

'I just thought you'd be interested,' said my mother, taking offence, 'but if you know it all already I needn't have bothered. All I can say is that she sounds a bit cracked, seeing nobody and living in that vast house.'

I don't know why it should have made me so angry. After all, Miss Barnaby would probably have considered it an honour to be called cracked.

'Not half as cracked as you,' I said furiously.

My mother was silent a moment, trying to think of something sufficiently biting to say. Then she thought of it.

'Well, one thing's certain anyway; she must be a very odd woman to take such an interest in you. Perhaps you make

67

yourself a little more lively and interesting when you are with her than you do at home.'

Miss Barnaby used to laugh when I complained to her about my mother. 'Grown-ups are the same the world over. They are always unreasonable. Why believe that they are superior beings? Instead they deserve our pity because they are too old to learn any better. Mind you learn what you can before you are past it.'

I wondered how old Miss Barnaby considered herself but I did not ask.

9

Popularity is not a virtue

Miss Barnaby seemed to take a great liking to Michael. I usually came alone on Saturday mornings to pick up Camouflage but in the afternoon sometimes Michael would come back with me. As the days grew shorter we would start back after lunch because Michael had to be home before dark. The road between Grewelthwaite and Bowden Farm was very lonely and Mrs Metcalfe did not like it if Michael was not back before nightfall. Miss Barnaby always offered us tea and cakes and would ask us how the day had passed. But there was also musical talk with Michael. I began to realise how much his violin meant to him. I know lots of girls who learn the piano, or sometimes other instruments, but they mostly seem to regard it as a drag, something their parents have imposed on them. When I had seen Michael coming out of the Grammar School with his violin, I merely thought, 'Oh, that's why he was staying late.' He had not talked to me about music, nor did I hear it mentioned much at home. He seemed rather shy about it. But to Miss Barnaby he would speak in a rush, with shining eyes, of pieces of music he liked playing, of things he had heard on the radio, and of his ambition to be a musician. He belonged to a local string orchestra; he hoped to get an audition for the National Youth Orchestra.

'I am glad to find a fellow enthusiast,' said Miss Barnaby. 'Some day I must hear you play.'

Michael was covered with confusion. 'I don't play like you,' he said. 'I mean, I'm not very good.'

Miss Barnaby laughed. 'Is that a refusal, or a display of false modesty?'

'It's not false modesty . . . I mean, of course, I'll play for you sometime but I don't want you to expect anything extraordinary.'

'Our Michael's always practising the violin now,' said Mrs Metcalfe. 'It's that Miss Barnaby o' yours. He wants to make a real good impression on her. He's scared to death o' making a fool o' himself in front of her. When's the great concert going to be, then?'

No great day had been fixed. I told Miss Barnaby how eager and frightened Michael was to play before her. She was surprised; 'I thought he didn't really want to,' she said.

This was one Saturday morning when I came to fetch Camouflage.

'Tell me about your friend Michael,' she said. 'I think he is one of the mad, a fellow countryman of ours.'

I told her all I knew about Michael. He is a rather silent boy, not given to talking about himself. At first I had been afraid that he would be ashamed of me before other Grammar School boys, but it didn't turn out that way. Anyway, he was usually alone. He has two sisters, but they are very much older than he is. One is married; the other is a teacher. His mother says he spends a lot of time wandering about the dale by himself. They used to have a dog who went with him everywhere but since he died they have not had the heart to replace him. 'He misses the company,' said Mrs Metcalfe. 'That's why he's so taken up wi' that Camouflage o' yours.'

'I think he must be a rather "reclusive" boy,' said Miss Barnaby, who was much taken by this word of Mrs Cousins. 'And music is not something which helps to make one friends amongst the Philistines. One spends so much time practising and, besides, they think one must be rather mad, or else putting it on, to take so much interest in something which bores them.'

'Is that what you found?'

'You know the inhabitants of Knaresley think, to put it politely, that I am rather eccentric.'

'But it must be very lonely to have no friends.'

'Oh, I have my own friends – there is no need to worry about me. The gossips of Knaresley think I see no one because I don't see them . . . but you know,' she added, after a pause, 'if you grow to be as old as I am, many of your friends die, and those that are left scatter far and wide. I have a friend in Canada, another one in New York. One who died recently used to live in Rome; I could visit her sometimes. But I still have a great friend who lives in Manchester; when I go to visit her we go on a musical spree – concerts every night if we can manage it. And some friends in Leeds too, quite close at hand.'

'But no friends in Knaresley.'

'There were one or two but they are dead. One must be a normal, gregarious person to be satisfied with the people nearest at hand for one's friends. Some people are like sheep and like living together in herds. Others, like cats, walk by themselves. It is sad that gregariousness is so highly thought of by everyone – I suppose because the sheep-people are easier to organise. I am always saddened when I hear the grand names they give the herd instinct – "Public spirit", "School spirit", "team spirit" – none of which I ever had despite being blamed for my "high spirits". Aren't these the qualities that your teachers praise?'

'Yes, you're right,' I said.

'These are the virtues of putting the good of the herd before the good of the individual and anyone can see the advantage of that to those in authority, like teachers. You are always telling me how they blame you for not making lots of friends, in other words for not fitting in, which is very inconvenient for them. But after all, popularity is not a virtue.'

'I suppose it isn't,' I said. 'They are always cross with me when everyone else has a partner and I haven't, or when they are choosing teams and I am the last one left out. Of course it's just because it's a nuisance to them.'

'Perhaps I shouldn't tell you things against all these well-meaning people whose only aim is to see you happy, to see you "fitting in", in other words, conforming and being just like them. You'd better not believe a word I say, or it will warp you for life I ought to be shut up for being an evil influence on youth, don't you think so?'

Since she was joking I told her a padded cell was the only thing.

'But seriously, Ruth, you don't have to be so upset when people blame you for being "unsociable" or whatever they call it. It does upset you, doesn't it?'

'But I should like to have friends, you know . . .'

'Of course, naturally. You have Michael already, and there will be many more. All I mean is that gregarious people think it's a virtue to make friends easily and have lots of them, just because we all think that other people would be better if they were just like us.'

'Then you think other people ought all to be reclusive like you?'

'Aha! You've caught me there – I'm afraid I probably do.' Then she went on, 'But there is a difference between Michael and us. I don't think he feels guilty for being solitary. It comes naturally to him – as it does to Camouflage. Do you remember how surprised he looked when I asked him what the other boys thought of his highbrow musical tastes and he said, "But what does it matter to me what people think?" As if it really had never bothered him.'

Michael did play for Miss Barnaby in the end. 'I played awfully,' he said to me afterwards. 'I was so ashamed. I couldn't do a thing right. Then she played something for me on the 'cello. When she is playing you forget everything else. I even forgot how badly I had played. Afterwards she made me play my piece again, and I played it marvellously, better than I've ever done it before. When I'd finished she said, "There's no need for me to praise you – you know how well you played and that should be a greater pleasure to you than any words of praise from me".'

Michael is not very talkative. On our walks he would be silent most of the time. When I look back at it I remember talking and talking myself, about Miss Barnaby, about my mother and all sorts of other things. He seemed to be listening. Sometimes he would say yes, or no, or make some short comment. Then suddenly he would stop and say 'Look!' I would stop talking and look. I had been so busy talking that I had scarcely noticed the scene around. Michael was not a great one for describing what he wanted you to look at. He just said 'look' and stood gazing with a slight smile on his face. Perhaps we had reached a point where we could overlook the whole dale. Through the serried ranks of clouds came here and there a shaft of sunlight, catching rising smoke far away in the distance or moving across the sides of the fell chasing the shadows before it. Again there was a place we sometimes went to where we could look back towards Knaresley and see the silhouette of the cathedral topping the town, and behind, the vale of York stretching as far as we could see except to the left, where, if the weather was clear, we could see the Hambletons, sometimes a pale whitish grey but more often blue, a clear cobalt or sometimes darker and purpler. I remember one day when a storm was approaching and the air was so clear that I could see every detail with sharp edges for miles and miles. The Hambletons were a deep purple and all the plain was in different shades of blue, and against this the grass of the near fell was lit with an orange light where the sun shone through the storm clouds. Michael stopped suddenly as the sunlight crept across the fell. 'Look!' he said.

It was getting too cold now to sit down and paint but sometimes I drew quickly in pencil in my sketchbook and painted it as soon as I got home before I forgot the colours. My mother said the one with the orange light was 'rather lurid'. I was pleased that Miss Barnaby liked it because I privately thought it was one of my best sketches.

I sometimes wonder, looking at Miss Barnaby's pictures,

whether my mother would disapprove of them as much as she does of Mrs Renton's. For instance, the calendars and Christmas cards of flowers which she keeps up year after year. It is so difficult to know what one ought to admire. Sometimes there are things which I think are just lovely, like *The Old Shepherd's Chief Mourner*, and then my mother snorts contemptuously. And whenever I go to put the tea things away at Miss Barnaby's and I see that great engraving of *The Stag at Bay* I wonder if that is sentimental too. I suppose my mother must be right, though sometimes I doubt it when she says there couldn't be an orange light and I know there was because I saw it. Miss Barnaby says I must choose for myself. 'Other people can't tell you what is beautiful, because it's different for different people.'

Miss Barnaby's house was as cold as a tomb in the winter. All those vast big rooms with high ceilings, and long corridors with stone floors – I don't know how they can ever have been warm even in the old days when Pa Barnaby was rich and there were lots of servants. Miss Barnaby didn't try to keep anything warm except the big sitting-room at the back where she lived. There she had three oil stoves of different sorts in far corners of the room and a coal fire in the grate. There was a screen before the door and another screen behind her chair and when she had closed the big wooden shutters and drawn the heavy fringed velvet curtains it was quite cosy. The dining-room, where *The Stag at Bay* hung, was arctic. In the music-room there was nothing but a gas fire, because, as she says, she gets very warm when she plays. I believe the gas lights used to make a bit of warmth and there were two or three more oil stoves to stop the pipes from freezing up. Michael and I used to help Miss Barnaby fill the stoves and we brought in coals for the fire. The man who delivered the paraffin used to help her too.

'You are very good to me,' she would say, 'and so is the paraffin man. I should never survive this winter without you.'

When Michael and I could not go by No Road for Motors because the river was too full – and all during the early months of the year it was very full – he took me and Camouflage by other ways. Sometimes we went further up the dale along the road which went past Bowden Farm and presently became a track. The dale became shallower and shallower and the beck became smaller and smaller; we passed the last tree, a magnificent ash which grew beside a barn at the water's edge, and beyond that was the open moor. Or he would take us up a little gill with rocky cliffs at the foot of which the stream had worn itself a course full of waterfalls, rapids and whirlpools. The whirlpools were in deep circular holes which the movement of the water had eaten out for itself in the limestone.

When we took her on new walks Camouflage was full of suspicion. She would follow us from Bowden Farm and seeing us take an unfamiliar turning she would hang back mewing questioningly.

'We're going this way today, Camouflage,' I would call to her.

She would proceed by a series of swift spurts when her head and tail would be in line with her body and her flanks rippling with the movement of her legs. Then she would stop, head raised, tail lowered, ears pricked, whiskers twitching and she would question the surrounding scenery with loud miaows. Then she would spurt forward again. If ever a rock or hillock presented a point of vantage she would race up it and stand poised as if she expected to spy an approaching enemy. And all the time she glanced back over her shoulder to see we were not followed. If anything suspicious occurred, like the movement of a sheep, she would bottlebrush her tail. She could make it so large and fluffy that she looked more like a grey squirrel than a cat.

We did not usually meet other people on our walks, but I remember one time when we met a man walking with his dog. Both Camouflage and the dog were taken by surprise; they rounded a rock and came face to face. But gone were the days when Camouflage was frightened of dogs. The animal was a large one, at least four times her size, but she made herself look as large as possible, standing sideways across the path, her back arched and all the hairs in the black stripe that ran along her spine standing on end, and her tail switching backwards and forwards above her like a huge erect bottlebrush, while she spat and growled and hissed. The dog looked pained and undecided. He thought it was best to pretend that he had intended to go round the other side of the rock. Camouflage was too fast for him; she met him half-way round in the same provocative manner. The dog withdrew gingerly and we had to pick Camouflage up and carry her, struggling like an eel and hissing and growling, until we were round a bend and out of sight. Even so, our intrepid heroine went running back, tail bristling, in an excess of eagerness to join battle. It was not until we had gone about half a mile further that her fur settled back into position and she stopped making forays backwards to make sure we were not being followed.

It was really wonderful how willing Camouflage was to get into her basket. I remember how Byron used to struggle and develop a hundred extra legs so that as soon as we had stuffed four inside we found that he had managed to force another three outside. At the very sight of his basket Byron would make himself scarce, while Camouflage was quite happy to sleep in it when it was left standing by the Aga at

Bowden Farm and when we shut the lid down she would mew a bit at first but presently would become resigned and silent. I remember one journey with Byron when he protested solidly for two hours.

10

When did you last see your father?

Michael knew the dale so well from having lived there all his life that he could have gone blindfold and he would still have known not only exactly where he stood, but exactly what he could see from that point; but when I tried to make a map of all the paths we took he was no good at all. He did not seem to be able to imagine what it would look like in plan. My own attempts were not very good and I wanted to buy a large-scale map which would show us just how things were laid out in relation to one another. There did not seem to be much chance of saving up for this since I had put my elbow through the stained glass in Mrs Renton's front door. 'It all has to be restored to its pristine glory,' said my mother sarcastically. 'You couldn't have committed a greater crime if you had put your elbow through one of the windows of Chartres.' But despite the fact that she thought the glass hideous she was very cross with me for breaking it and told Mrs Renton that she couldn't understand how I was growing up such a little hooligan and of course I should pay for its replacement out of my pocket money. Grown-ups are two-faced.

But I managed to get a map in a most unexpected manner.

It was late in February, I think. It was during an art lesson. A prefect came in and spoke to the Art Mistress. The head-mistress wanted to see me. What on earth had I done? With trembling hand I knocked at her door. 'Come in' sounded from inside. I entered. Some man was sitting talking to her. He turned and smiled at me. It was my father.

I don't suppose I looked overjoyed to see him. After all, I had never heard from him since he went away. He didn't send me anything for my birthday or Christmas. Not that I want to appear grasping; I wouldn't have minded about there being no presents but it looked as if he'd forgotten that I even existed. I just said 'Hullo'.

'Ruth seems to have settled down very well here, Mr Wintersgill,' the headmistress said rather stiffly.

'You are quite happy?' asked my father.

'Yes,' I said.

There was an awkward silence.

'You like living in the country?' he asked.

'Oh, rather!'

He smiled. 'Your Mother wrote and told me you liked it here and wouldn't want to move back to Horsepath. I thought perhaps she was bluffing.' Then he added, 'I daresay you miss Byron more than me.'

'I do like being in the country,' I said. 'Besides, I've got another cat.'

'But Mrs Raines told me your landlady didn't allow pets.'

'This cat belongs to a friend of mine, you see. Did you go to see Mrs Raines?'

'Yes, Byron is thriving. I don't think he misses you. Not the way I do.'

I didn't say anything. The headmistress asked me if I had made any friends.

'Yes,' I said, 'but they're not at this school.'

The headmistress was obviously annoyed at my saying that because she liked to think that I had 'settled down well'.

'Your form mistress told me you were fitting in better this term,' she said sternly.

'Oh, I'm all right,' I said. 'I'm not gregarious by nature.'

The headmistress looked very disapproving but my father laughed. 'Well,' he said, 'I'm glad to see you looking so healthy. I mustn't keep you any longer away from your lessons. Is there any little thing you'd like by way of a present? Your mother was so angry with me before that she sent back the things I sent for your birthday and Christmas.'

I was so astonished to hear that he had sent me presents before that I couldn't think of anything to ask for. So he hadn't really forgotten about me. It was all a misunderstanding. Then I remembered the map.

'A really big-scale map,' I said, 'that shows footpaths. I want one that shows Grewelthwaite and Bowden Beck and all the part round there.'

'I'll see what I can find,' he said. We had all stood up by now, ready to depart. He kissed me on the top of the head. 'My dear little Ruth,' he said. I wanted to say, 'My dear little Daddy,' but somehow it isn't the sort of thing one says in front of the headmistress. When I got back to the classroom I kept wishing I'd said it. I'd been so beastly to him. I went over and over the conversation. Mummy had written and told him I didn't want to go back to Horsepath. And, of course, that meant back to him. He thought perhaps she was bluffing, that perhaps it wasn't true. And I had said it was true. He'd said 'I daresay you miss Byron more than me' and I didn't say 'No'. He'd said how he missed me and I didn't say anything at all. It was all because I thought he'd forgotten about me and didn't want me. It was all because of a lie.

I hated my mother for sending the presents back, for telling me he didn't want me, for letting me think he'd forgotten me. I suddenly remembered that time she'd been so cross with me for fetching the letters in the morning and had made me promise not to do it again. Perhaps he'd written me letters and she'd sent them back. If only I'd known then I wouldn't have been so beastly to him. I'd have looked pleased to see him.

To think that Miss Barnaby had guessed it was a lie and I hadn't believed her. I couldn't really believe that my mother would tell me a lie. And then, Miss Barnaby hadn't guessed about the presents and the letters and without them it did look as if what my mother said was true. I felt so mad with my mother. I would tell her what I thought of her, when I got home. That's what I thought. I'll tell her I hate her because she told me a lie.

When I went home after school, as I went up the stairs in Mrs Renton's house, I found myself staring at the picture *When did you last see your father?* Isn't it funny? I hadn't noticed it for months but it had to catch my eye just that day. I felt horribly guilty and expected to find my mother looking over my shoulder. I ran up to our room and started doing my homework so as to think of something else. But I kept on thinking she would come in suddenly and ask me that question. My indignation began to dwindle. I knew I would never have the courage to tell her what I thought of her. I'm like my father really, I hate scenes. He ran away and left us so as to avoid scenes. And I probably wouldn't tell my mother I'd seen him, so as to avoid a scene.

But somebody ought to tell her it was wrong to have done that. Somebody ought to make her feel it was wrong to tell me that lie. Who? Miss Barnaby? But, no. I remembered Miss Barnaby saying, 'Wouldn't you have done the same?' 'Your poor mother,' she had said, 'you shouldn't have told her you'd rather live with your father.'

I wouldn't tell my mother I hated her. It wasn't just to avoid a scene. I couldn't tell her I loved her but it was a bit hard to tell her I hated her. One has to make allowances.

My mother did not come in until much later than usual. She was in a funny mood – frightfully impatient and irritable at one moment and then very apologetic and affectionate the next. I did not know what to make of it. Everything I did was wrong and then a moment later she was all over me asking me if I was really happy here in Knaresley. When I assured her I liked Knaresley very much she said, 'But I can't understand why you haven't made any little friends.' Always the same old criticism.

'There's Michael,' I said.

'Yes,' she said, 'there's Michael.' She had begun to approve of Michael because she had heard about him from her colleagues in the staff room, how he belonged to this string orchestra I mentioned, and what high hopes his music teacher had of him. 'But you're not very musical,' she said in a puzzled manner. 'Oh well, I'm sure it's very educational for you to be exposed to musical people like him and Miss Barnaby. Who knows what latent talents it may bring out.' She didn't get on with Michael herself because he was shy and said nothing in her presence. 'Does your friend never utter?' she asked me. But

Michael seemed to get on all right without talking very much and he seemed to be perfectly contented without having dozens of friends. It was a great comfort to me to know I wasn't the only one. He really wasn't gregarious by nature but I came to the conclusion in the end that it didn't come so naturally to me. It was just as Miss Barnaby had said. 'You and I are solitary by force of circumstance. Michael was born that way. It does not worry him. He is scarcely aware of it.'

When I had gone to bed on the day I had seen my father, my mother came in and sat on the foot of the bed. 'Knaresley wouldn't be so bad if we didn't have to live in this dump, would it?' she said.

'But I like Knaresley.'

Then she got cross. 'Do you imagine I like living with Mrs Renton? Oh, I can assure you I positively adore placating her when you've stuck your elbow through her atrocious stained glass! There's nothing I enjoy more than the sight of her jolly furniture, not to speak of her pictures!' Then she stopped herself and started being affectionate again. 'You had lots of little friends at Horsepath. Are you sure you weren't happier there?'

'We're not going back to live in Horsepath, are we?' I asked in horror. I realised suddenly how much I did like Knaresley and the dale, Michael and Miss Barnaby, Camouflage and No Road for Motors. I realised that I had forgotten all my 'little' friends of six months before; I was shocked that I felt so little desire to see them again. But I couldn't feel very enthusiastic about it.

'No, no,' said my mother, 'I wasn't thinking of going back there. I'm glad you like Knaresley. I'm glad you like the country.'

'Oh, I do like the country,' I said with enthusiasm.

'So I gather. Your father gave me this to give to you.'

84

And she got up briskly and went out, leaving the map in my hands.

Well, well. So she knew all along when I had last seen my father. She must have seen him herself before she came home. But she wouldn't say anything about it. It had never occurred to me, when she kept on asking did I like Knaresley and was I sure I didn't want to go back to Horsepath, that this could have been because she had been talking to him about the same things.

I hadn't realised when I'd said, 'We're not going back to live in Horsepath, are we?' in tones of horror, that it had meant to her, 'We're not going back to live with Daddy, are we?' I felt cross with her for getting me to imply that, when I didn't mean it at all. I lay tossing about in bed for a long time, feeling mad with my mother and hating her, all over again. Then suddenly I began laughing to myself. I couldn't have planned it better if I'd known what I'd been doing! With my mother you've got to pretend to want the opposite thing to what you do want. If you say you want to wear your sandals, she's sure to insist that you wear your Wellingtons. If, on the other hand, you say, 'Perhaps I'd better wear my Wellingtons today,' she'll exclaim, 'Whatever for? I'd wear my sandals if I were you.' So, I thought, if she thinks I don't want to go back to live with Daddy, she'll decide it would be much better for us if we did.

Still, I wished I could have explained it to Daddy. I mean, why I'd been so horrid to him.

'I wish I'd known he'd sent those presents,' I said to Miss Barnaby.

'Ah, well,' she said, 'I daresay you'll be seeing him again.'

'Do you think we'll go back to live in Horsepath?' I asked her.

'I've never met your mother and I've never met your father, so how can I tell? Are you really so sure you don't want to go back there? You must have had friends.'

'But I like it here,' I said obstinately. 'Anyway, I've got friends here now. You and Michael.'

'You could always come and visit us,' she said.

'It wouldn't be the same. Besides you don't know what it was like in the old days. They were always having rows.'

'But your mother would be happier with a house of her own.'

'She hated the house.'

'And you've told me she doesn't like teaching at the Modern school.'

'That was at the beginning. I believe she likes it now.'

'So you're inclined to think that it would be better if your parents stayed apart? I should have thought . . .'

But then she stopped. 'I really must try to stop influencing you. Camouflage,' she said to her, 'you've let me do it again.' Camouflage, who had fallen asleep in a half-sitting position, pricked up her ears and said M-riaow. She sounded just like my mother saying 'What is it?' when I interrupt her reading a book.

'She was having a very absorbing dream and we have spoilt it,' I said.

As I was going she said to me, 'Just think how nice it would be to leave Marion Renton's and have a home and a cat of your own.'

'Camouflage is different from other cats,' I said. 'I don't want another one.'

11

Pros and Cons

Well, I thought, all those stories about sweet little children reuniting divorced parents, like that one about the twins that they turned into a film with Hayley Mills playing both twins, it's just not like life, I thought. I mean, I thought that story was quite good when I first read it, but now, well, it was just unrealistic. Anyway, it wasn't like my mother and father. Whatever Miss Barnaby thought, she didn't know what it had been like before Daddy went away. Not that he was there often, as I said before. But they used to quarrel all the time. It is painful to remember. What is the point of going back to that? It is such a long time now since Mummy really lost her temper, that I had almost forgotten what it was like. I think she has really been much happier since she got over the first shock. During the first few weeks before we left Horsepath, she was angry all the time, almost as if anything anyone said to her was an insult; like not telling me we were going to move and then being angry because I didn't know. Or with Byron, saying abruptly that he would have to be put down, just because I asked what would become of him, seeing Mrs Renton wouldn't have cats. 'That cat's all you care about! You expect everything to be planned around him' – which I didn't. I should have thought it was quite natural to ask what was to become of him.

When we first came to Knaresley she was still a bit that way inclined. She hated Mrs Renton's and she hated the Modern school and sometimes she behaved as if it was all my fault we had come there and as if I was responsible for the bad behaviour of the pupils in her class who were always playing her up. It was then she kept on nagging me about not having any friends. 'I can't think why you don't behave like normal children of your age, instead of moping and wandering about by yourself,' she would grumble; then at other times she would say in a worried voice, 'I don't want you to be lonely or unhappy. Isn't there anyone in your class you'd like to bring home sometimes? Though I suppose this house is a pretty unwelcoming place.' This was the sort of thing she would say when she came to sit on my bed at night before tucking me in and turning the lights off.

At the time I did not notice the change but looking back I can see that all this – her irritation in particular – belongs to the first few months we were living here. Then we got used to Mrs Renton's furniture, Mummy got used to her pupils' insolence, or else they got less insolent and her bouts of bad temper grew further and further apart. It was only when I tried to remember what it was like when we first arrived that I realised how happy we had been for a long time since. Happy, perhaps, is the wrong word. I had stopped being miserable, that was all. And so had she.

I don't really understand grown-ups, but I think she had begun to enjoy teaching. 'It's much better for a woman to have a job,' she said to me. 'I'm glad you've found an interest.' (She meant painting.) 'I gave up everything when I married; I thought it would be nice not to have to work for my living. Don't you make that mistake.' Mummy used often to talk to me like that, telling me the things not to do when I was grown up, which were always the things that she had done. 'You'll know when you're as old as I am,' she would say. 'It pays to have an interest and it pays to keep it up. Don't throw it over for anyone. People aren't worth it.'

Then there was the fact that Thursday afternoons when she took 4C, which used to be the black spot of the week, became a time when she was often in high spirits and would make something special for supper and say to me, 'Knaresley isn't such a bad place after all, is it?' It was odd that I hadn't noticed when the change took place.

Why should people think it was necessarily a 'good thing' for Mummy to give up her job and go back to 'that barrack' in Horsepath, because even if she didn't like Mrs Renton's she had hated our old house? 'What I should like,' she said, 'would be a little house that I could plan and decorate and modernise just the way I wanted it. That would be fun, wouldn't it? A little house in Knaresley or just outside, because you do like living in Knaresley, don't you?' Yes, that would be nice, I thought. People are wrong, I thought. She wouldn't be happier going back to the old life. Miss Barnaby shrugged her shoulders. 'Perhaps you're right,' she said. 'Far be it from me to interfere in matters of which I know so little. Anyway, this appears to have been a false alarm.'

Because I hadn't seen any more of my father.

Those first few weeks after his fateful appearance in our midst, I lived in perpetual expectation. I went upstairs with averted face. Passing that picture was like passing a burglar alarm. When my mother came in I pretended to be buried in my homework and I did not dare look up until I felt sure the atmosphere was quite normal and that nothing had happened. Which, day after day, it hadn't. He wasn't mentioned. One day Mummy said the bit about the little house of our own, but otherwise she did not ask me again about whether I liked living in Knaresley.

Each weekend that nothing had happened was like a reprieve. We weren't going back to Horsepath yet. Another weekend in which I could go exploring the dale with Michael. Now that we had the map and I could see the shapes of the mountains and all the names of places which I tried to picture to myself from the sound of the words – Brittlewell and Brittleside, Keddraw Falls and Aysdale Scar, Gellowgill and Simnelwater – all these places which I might never see if I were to be snatched away so soon; now I persuaded Michael to abandon the familiar walks, all starting from Bowden Farm, and we would go off on bicycles to see some place he had never been to before, just because I liked the sound of the name, or because the contours all came close together on the map so that we could tell it must be very steep and craggy. Camouflage did not always come with us, but if the bicycle ride was not too long, we would take her. I don't think she always enjoyed exploring unfamiliar places and we did not like to lose sight of her because how would she find her way back? But I very much wanted to see these places, especially since I was so uncertain about what was going to happen. I must have talked endlessly about the pros and cons, whether we should go back to Daddy or not, both to Miss Barnaby, and to Michael, who never offered an opinion on this matter. Yet I'm sure he listened to every word I said so it was better than confiding in Byron. But it must have been very tedious for him. I remember one day we were trudging up some track together and I was worrying away at the same old subject.

'You see,' I said, 'it's not that I don't want to see Daddy again, for myself. I was so horrid to him that time he came to school. And I've never even thanked him for the map or told him why I didn't seem pleased to see him. If only I could write him a letter, but I daren't ask my mother for his address. I ought to have written long ago, only I thought something was going to happen, I thought I'd be seeing him again. Every time I came home from school, or when Mummy opened her letters in the morning, I expected there'd be news . . .'

I must have run out of breath, talking and going uphill. Michael reached the top first and stood looking back over the dale. When I reached him he said, as if it was something profound and wise, 'You know, it's like the weather.'

What was he talking about? 'What's like the weather?' I asked crossly.

Michael dug his hands into his pockets and frowned at the view. 'Well, it's like this,' he said. 'Sometimes I spend hours' (and he drew the word out so that it went on for ever) – 'h-o-u-rs trying to make up my mind whether I want it to be a fine day or a rainy day tomorrow.

'I don't mean,' he added hastily, 'that your Mum and Dad's like the weather. It's just that – 'and he frowned even more deeply searching for the words – 'just that it doesn't make any difference to the weather.'

Michael was right, of course. And it was so difficult to decide what was the best thing that in the end it was a relief, (as well as a disappointment) to find that there was nothing to be decided, or rather, that everything was going to go on just the same whatever I decided, and that nothing was going to happen just because I wanted it to, or, for that matter, because I didn't want it to.

12

A week in Horsepath

So the Easter holidays arrived and nothing had happened. A
friend of mine from Horsepath days had written to ask me
to stay for a week. Mummy seemed very pleased. 'That will
be fun for you,' she said. 'Aren't you pleased?'

'I suppose so,' I said.

'But I thought Sally Collins used to be your best friend?'

'Yes, she was. Yes,' I added, 'yes, it will be fun to see her
again.'

But it was not until I found that Michael was going on a
musical course during this same week that I managed to work
up any enthusiasm about this visit to Sally. It was convenient
that she had asked me just when he would be away and I would
not be able to go up the dale because my mother would not
let me go all by myself. And then I began to look forward to
seeing my old friends again and telling them all about Michael
and Camouflage and Miss Barnaby. Little did I think that I

would never want to mention a word about any of these once I got there!

I went by bus to Horsepath. Sally was waiting at the bus stop to meet me. I almost didn't recognise her. She had always been rather tall but I hadn't expected her to look so much older than me. She was wearing a shift dress in lilac-coloured courtelle and nylon stockings and her shoes weren't actually high-heeled but they had very pointed toes and a little strap across the instep which made them look frightfully grown-up. She was shivering a bit and pretending not to be cold and she did not seem very pleased to see me. 'Your bus was late,' she said.

'I hope you haven't been waiting long in the cold,' I said. She was jumping up and down a bit because of the cold and stopped herself, probably remembering that grown-ups don't hop, skip and jump.

'It is a bit chilly,' she said.

I didn't say she was a fool not to have put her coat on and I soon found out that she never wore her coat if she could help it because she thought it was a childish pattern. She was always badgering her mother to get her a smarter, more 'with-it' coat, but Mrs Collins only said, 'You're shooting up so fast, dear, it would be madness to buy you a coat at the end of the winter.'

I couldn't think of a thing to say to Sally as we walked back from the bus stop. I was just so embarrassed about my old mac which was getting rather tight under the arms, and my socks, and my sensible walking shoes.

When we got to the house Sally went into the living-room and turned on the radio and flung herself down in an armchair. She left it to Mrs Collins to show me up to my room and there I spent as long as possible slowly unpacking my things and trying to make myself hope that I would find some astonishing garment that I didn't know I had put in, nor even possessed, so that I could go downstairs changed and acceptable. But there were just my own old clothes. In order to put off going downstairs I pressed my nose against the window-pane. A few far-between raindrops were lashing against the glass. Well, that was one comfort; if it rained, at least I could not regret not being up the dale. To think Sally Collins and I had been friends until last summer, fooling around climbing trees and cooking sausages over a fire in the garden and, at her request, I would tell her interminable stories about knights and ladies in improbable medieval wars, walking round and round the playground during the dinner-hour. I found I had tears in my eyes so I went to the bathroom and dipped my face in cold water and rubbed it hard with a towel and then ventured downstairs.

Sally had a record on the gramophone and she took no notice of me for a long time. At last she asked me if I liked the Rolling Stones. We don't have telly or a gramophone, and my mother doesn't have the radio on unless she wants to listen to something, but I tried to hide my ignorance and she began to get a little friendly.

'I suppose Knaresley is pretty square,' she said.

'I suppose it is.'

'I'll show you a few things while you're here.'

'Please do.'

'You could always borrow a pair of my shoes,' she added thoughtfully.

At last teatime arrived. I came to look forward to mealtimes so much during that week because they were stakes that marked off the passing of time. Lunch meant that yet another morning was over and tea that the bulk of another day had been disposed of. And after tea came telly which was another blessing because it took one's mind off the long drag of finding something to do.

Sally did lend me a pair of her shoes. She didn't trust me with her stockings but she made me go barelegged because 'socks look silly', she said. We went to do some shopping for her mother and afterwards we went to a coffee bar and had milkshakes. I had never had one before so I was quite curious to find out what they were like, but it was a great disappointment really. And the funny thing was that Sally couldn't stand milk and always used to get someone else, usually me, to drink hers at school. There was a juke box in this coffee bar but we hadn't any money to put into it; I was quite glad because it seemed an awful waste when we could go home and listen to Sally's records if we wanted to. But Sally went and examined it and told me all the songs she thought were 'great' and I pretended to know what she was talking about. Presently there came in a group of youths who crowded round the juke box, putting money in and choosing records. She tried to get them to choose the ones she liked but no one took much notice of her until one lad called out, 'Hey, and what about the other kid – what do *you* want?'

I was still sitting isolated on my high stool and I blushed horribly and stammered, 'I don't know.' I had forgotten all the names of the songs.

'Come on,' he said, 'what do you like?'

'I like the Rolling Stones,' I said because it was the only name I could remember. For some reason everyone laughed at me. I never found out why. Sally took me away immediately. She was in high dudgeon.

'You look such a baby,' she said.

As we went home she told me how boring it must be in

Knaresley. 'Whatever do you do with yourself?' she asked.

She was most impressed when I told her about Michael because she thought he was a boyfriend. 'Actually,' I said, 'he's not really a boyfriend, he's just a friend who happens to be a boy.' Immediately after I'd said that I wished I hadn't but then afterwards I decided it didn't matter because she didn't know the difference. Michael sent me a postcard while I was there which told me all about the bits of music they were playing on his course and other technical things which neither she nor I understood, but she was quite stunned that I should receive a postcard from a real boy.

How many times during that week I wished I had some moderately grown-up, smart-looking clothes. My mother was always complaining that I took no interest in clothes because I just liked a sweater and jeans or something I could muck around in, and always felt stupid in my best dress which she had made for me and which I was always pulling down at the front because the neck was uncomfortable, and she would come up behind me in annoyance and give a sharp tug at the waist-line which nearly throttled me. Clothes, in fact, were one of the bones of contention between my mother and me. Whatever I put on, which was always for comfort or convenience, the only sensible reason I can see for selecting clothes, was always the wrong combination of colours in her eyes, or it bulged or something. 'I cannot have you going out like that,' was what she was always saying.

Now I know it's stupid for someone with my ideas about clothes to develop a yearning for that smooth well-groomed look, as Sally's fashion mags put it, knowing all the time that I'd feel a trussed up fool in such a get-up. But it was absolute misery to wear my shapeless tweed skirt and one time favourite jumper while Sally displayed her latest triumph, a trouser suit in a stinging shade of apple green or a very sophisticated mini-dress with ruffles at the neck and cuffs, in shocking pink, orange and lilac that one could scarcely look at without feeling dizzy. 'It's called op,' she said. You can imagine what my afore-mentioned best dress looked like next to that. It's Viyella, dark green and brown, with long sleeves and high neck, and a gathered skirt. With sandals and ankle socks to complete the picture and remembering too that I am pulling it about all the time because the wretched neck is so uncomfortable, I must have cut a charming figure at the tea party that was given in my honour. Most of my old friends were invited to this, and I am glad to say that they were not all so startlingly changed as Sally. Some of them still wore moderately childish clothes. I felt hopeful. They asked politely after my new life in Knares-ley; I plunged in. Someone at the other end of the table was talking about something else; my two neighbours tried to listen politely to me, but even I could see that they were more interested in the conversation in progress on the other side of them. Soon their opportunity came to join it and no one was listening to me any longer. I tried to find out what they were talking about, but since I had been placed at one end of a long narrow table, I only caught snatches of the conversation. It was about some character I had never heard of, who turned out to be a girl who had come since I had left. Nobody bothered to explain anything to me. My neighbours were leaning out across the table with their backs turned to me. Somebody was whispering something and two or three people started shaking with laughter. The joke was passed on. More people joined in the laughter. 'Tell me, tell me,' I begged.

'You don't know the people,' they said, 'you wouldn't find it funny.'

I was mortified. I wondered if they were laughing at me.

I won't bother to tell you all about the rest of that party. That night in bed I started to cry and I couldn't stop. Mrs Collins heard me and came in and was frightfully kind and comforting. Afterwards I heard her talking to Sally in the next room. I felt sure they were talking about me and I felt very embarrassed. Suddenly I heard Sally's voice raised. Her mother hushed her, but she went on. 'I don't care if she does hear,' she exclaimed. '*I* didn't want to have her!'

Her mother went on talking away in a quiet voice and then Sally broke in again, '*I* can't help it if her mother asked you to invite her . . .'

I buried my head in the pillow to prevent myself hearing anything more. I'd thought Sally had invited me herself. I had thought people actually wanted to see me again. I could have killed my mother. Oh, it wasn't fair! I would never have gone there if I had known it was like that, and now I had to stay two more whole days because my mother had gone away, and wasn't coming to fetch me till then. It's so mortifying, it's so mortifying, it's so mortifying, I said to myself because saying it over and over again gave me no time to start crying and I didn't want my sobs to be heard once more. I must have gone to sleep because next thing I knew I was waking up in the morning and I thought to myself, 'What's the matter? What's happened?' and then suddenly I remembered and I was so *mortified* that I blushed all over and winced although there was nobody there to see me. However, I didn't feel like crying, I just felt bitter. It wasn't fair.

13

For sale

With a stiff upper lip I managed to get through those next two days. One blessing was that Mrs Raines had asked me to tea so that I was able to get away from the Collinses for a whole afternoon. I was looking forward to seeing Byron again. Not that I imagined that he would greet me with the affection of the old Shepherd's Chief mourner; I knew my father was probably right when he said Byron wasn't missing me. Still, it would be nice to see my old Pussy again, and tell him all my troubles, even if he did fall asleep as soon as I started.

In fact I did enjoy seeing Byron again, and Mrs Raines too, because she is a very jolly kindly sort of person and drank in eagerly everything I could tell her about Mrs Renton and her house and Camouflage and how my mum was. 'I'm real sorry for your mum,' she said. 'I mean she had her faults like all of us, but she was a nice lady and most considerate.' (Which surprised me because I always thought my mother shouted at Mrs

Raines and found fault with her the whole time). 'You don't find many ladies like her nowadays. Your Dad, he came to see me, did you know? He was a nice gentleman too, always a good sort. Pity he was away such a lot. Yes,' she said, 'it was a great pity. And you, dearie, you're settling down all right? Made some new friends? She's even met a new pussy,' she added, addressing Byron, and tickling his stomach. He stretched and curled his paws and rolled over slightly without bothering to wake up.

'You don't know how he misses you,' she said; but I didn't believe her.

The awful thing was, Byron was so ugly. I never remembered him as being so thick and heavily built and cumbersome. He toddled about, he had none of that alertness nor agility that I had got used to with Camouflage. People talk about cats being graceful but he certainly wasn't. Of course he was getting old now. His ears had been battered in many fights which only added to the flat blob-like appearance of his face. Camouflage's face comes to a sharp point at her nose, and to two more sharp points at her ears, which gives her an appearance of liveliness and intelligence and fits in with her streamlined body. It is awful to think that one's affections can be so much influenced by mere good looks; I mean I thought I would always love dear old Byron but somehow I didn't regret at all having lost him because Camouflage was so much more beautiful.

On the way back from Mrs Raines I went round by our old house. I walked very slowly because I did not want to get back to the Collinses sooner than I needed, and as I walked along I was thinking what bliss it was going to be tomorrow when my mother came to fetch me, and what a blessing it was that we weren't coming back to live in Horsepath after all, since even Byron wasn't a great draw now. When I came round the corner of the street and saw 'that barrack' I began to feel nostalgic, I don't know why. Then I saw the 'For Sale' notice. I just stood still and suddenly I felt cold all over. A lump came in my throat and a tear or two trickled down my cheeks. Nobody had told me they were selling the house, our dear old house. Nobody told me anything.

I pulled myself together and walked on down the street very, very slowly. I ought to be glad. I didn't want to come back to Horsepath. But I didn't actually feel very glad. In fact I felt miserable.

The next morning my mother came to fetch me. What a relief. Mrs Collins gave her a cup of coffee. Sally was wearing her trouser suit and being quite nice because she would soon be rid of me, but as we left the house I heard her put one of her pop records on very loud and through the sitting-room window I caught a glimpse of her dancing jubilantly.

My mother said to me as we walked to the bus stop, 'That was a very strange garment Sally had on.'

'Didn't you like it?' I asked.

'It looked rather cheap and badly made. Besides Sally looked ridiculous in it.'

'She has such grown-up clothes,' I said regretfully.

'You wouldn't want to wear clothes like that,' my mother exclaimed. 'You, who don't care what you look like!'

'No, I suppose not,' I said sadly. 'They've all got so different – wearing nylons and make-up.'

Then my mother squeezed my arm and said, 'I'm glad I've got a sensible little girl,' and I felt all warm inside as if she and I stood united against a hostile world. I wondered if I should mention the old house to her or if it would make her cross and spoil a good moment. I asked all the same; at least I said, 'I went past our old house and I saw the "For Sale" notice in the garden,' trying to imply that it had not been a surprise in case she should be angry with me for not having known about it.

'Nobody wants to buy it, and I don't blame them,' she said. 'I can't imagine anyone *choosing* to live in that barrack.' Then she squeezed my arm once more and said affectionately, 'You don't want to live in Horsepath again, do you?'

'No.' I shook my head.

'I thought perhaps when you saw all your old friends again you'd change your mind.'

We climbed on to the top of the bus and when we had settled in Mummy started rootling in her bag. 'I've got something for you here,' she said. 'Ah, here it is. From your father.'

She handed me a chocolate Easter egg. Now was the moment; what should I say? What question should I ask about him that couldn't make her cross? 'That was very kind of him,' I said, putting off the moment. 'Let's eat some.'

When we had eaten some of the chocolate she exclaimed, 'I told him you'd never notice!'

'What?' I asked, guilty and puzzled.

'He insisted on putting it inside the egg and putting all the wrappings back as if it had never been touched. I told him you'd never notice, but of course he knew better.'

Still puzzled, I examined the paper packing from inside the egg. Wrapped up inside it I found a pocket compass.

'To use with your map,' said my mother grinning. 'Do you like it?'

'It's lovely.'

'Well, aren't you going to ask after him?' There was a trace of impatience in her voice, just a hint of 'All you think about is that cat.' I never manage to do the right thing. 'How is he?' I asked.

'Just like he always is.'

'Where's he living?'

'Oh, some wretched lodgings where the landlady spoils him. Trust a man to fall on his feet, while we get landed with Mrs Renton. We went to London for the week.' She hugged herself and grinned. 'You haven't said what you think of my new coat.'

I had thought it was new but usually when I say, 'Is that a new coat (hat, dress, etc.)?' she snorts, 'Had it for donkeys' years. Where would I get the money from for new clothes?'

'It's nice,' I said. 'Got it in London?'

She nodded. 'And shoes, too,' she said, stretching out her toes for admiration.

'They look nice, too.' I said. I couldn't think of any other admiring words. So that's why I was shoved off to the Collinses, I was thinking. She wanted me out of the way. 'I hope you had a nice time,' I said, hoping my goodwill did not sound too hollow. But she didn't notice.

'Marvellous!' she said. 'It's years since I've been up to London. Years since he's taken me to the theatre, or even the cinema.' (That was one of the things she used to get angry about, but as soon as he suggested anything she'd say she'd got a headache or she hadn't got a babysitter.) 'We had a splendid time. There was so much to see, so much to do . . .' and then suddenly remembering that I hadn't had such a good time, 'I'm sorry you didn't enjoy yourself, darling. I thought it would cheer you up to see your old friends. You seem to lead such a lonely life in Knaresley.'

'I didn't need cheering up,' I said. 'I'm perfectly happy in Knaresley.' I said that without thinking but as soon as I'd said it I felt an aching empty feeling in my mind. For a moment I couldn't remember why and then it flashed back into my mind – the For Sale notice. They were selling our old home. We couldn't be going back to Daddy, then. And yet Mummy had gone for a holiday with him, without me. It didn't add up somehow. I longed to know what was the right question to ask, but I dreaded asking the wrong one. Meanwhile, my mother was speaking.

'I'm so glad you like Knaresley, because I like Knaresley too. If only we didn't have to live at Mrs Renton's, if we could have a little house of our own, it would be perfect, wouldn't it?' And she patted my hand and added, 'Another time I'll take you up to London too, when you're a bit older.'

She was in such a jolly mood that I didn't dare speak in case I spoiled it. I'd ask Miss Barnaby what she thought. After all, she must know more about grown-ups than I do.

14

Left out

There was a note from Miss Barnaby waiting at Mrs Renton's, asking me to come round to tea. Michael was coming too, she wrote. He had come back from his course the day before and she had seen him already. I felt a tiny bit left out, but I had forgotten all about it when I went round to Palace Road that afternoon.

Michael was already there. He and Miss Barnaby were deep in conversation about music when I arrived but, 'We mustn't bore you,' said Miss Barnaby. 'Tell us what you've been doing. Did you have a good time?'

'No, horrid,' I said. 'They'd all changed, my friends.'

I found I didn't want to tell them all about it. When Miss

Barnaby wanted to know how they had changed, all I would say was, 'They all wore grown-up clothes and talked about people I didn't know.' Then I said to Camouflage. 'I went to visit my old pussy but he's not nearly as beautiful as you.'

'Poor old Byron. You used to think such a lot of him,' said Miss Barnaby.

I tickled Camouflage under the chin (she had been asleep in a chair by the fire), until she purred so loudly that you could hear her over the other side of the room.

'She's very susceptible to flattery,' said Miss Barnaby.

'And after I'd been to see him I walked back past our house. It's for sale. I didn't know before.'

After that we had tea and they started talking about music again. Naturally I couldn't join in so I just talked to Camouflage, who came and sat on my lap, and told her what a beautiful pussy she was and then I felt I had to tell her what a dear old pussy Byron had been or else it would be disloyal, though obviously she hadn't an idea what I was talking about. Eventually I got bored talking nonsense so I started listening to the musical conversation again. They were talking, I discovered with surprise, about a concert in Leeds to which it appeared they were both planning to go. Miss Barnaby realised I was listening so she explained. 'Michael and I have been planning this little outing. I managed to get two seats to hear Jacqueline Dupré playing.'

'I've never been to a real concert before,' said Michael, his eyes shining. 'It's awfully kind of Miss Barnaby.'

I felt so jealous I couldn't think of anything to say. I know I'm not interested in music and I only wanted to go to the concert because they were going and why should I expect Miss Barnaby to buy a ticket for me? I didn't expect her to buy me a ticket and I didn't even want to go to the concert. Did I want to stop them going? No, I didn't want that either. It was just – well, I felt left out.

'How nice,' I said.

When we left, Miss Barnaby said to me, 'Come and see me again, and tell me properly about your holiday in Horsepath. I'm afraid we were very preoccupied with our musical plans today.'

As we rode off together, Michael said, 'You'll come up to the farm and see us, won't you?' He sounded a little apologetic.

'Depends on the weather,' I said. He could ask me properly if he wanted to see me. I'd had enough of foisting myself on people who didn't care for my company.

'I'm sorry you had a rotten time with your friend,' he said.

'Oh, it was all right.' I didn't want him being sorry for me. He didn't say anything about the concert. He hung about at my gate but we had nothing to say to one another. He kept on saying, 'I must be going' and 'my mother will be wondering what's become of me' and at last he went, calling over his shoulder,

'Be seeing you!'

I was determined to get a better invitation than that before I went to Bowden Farm again, so the next day, which was gloriously fine, I took a packed lunch and my painting things and I went up to Grewelthwaite on my bicycle. I did not even take Camouflage with me because I didn't want to go round to see Miss Barnaby.

I thought I would do a large painting of the waterfall at Grewelthwaite because my mother had made me promise not to go up on the fell by myself so if Michael was not there I had to stick near the village. I had done a little sketch in my pocket sketch book but when I tried to paint it bigger in the Art class at school all the rocks looked like bundles piled up with dust sheets thrown over them and not like rocks at all. So I thought if I went and painted it big on the spot I could see how the rocks really went and not have to make them up.

Despite the sunshine above, down in the wooded hollow where the waterfall was it was cold and dank. I drew in the rocks and the trees which hang over the top closing it in like a cave. The waterfall was very full because of the recent rains and came churning down through the gap like milky coffee. The water in the pool was turbid and a deep brown in colour – very different from the weak china tea colour it has when there is less water coming down. I saw nobody at all, although there is a little footbridge just below the waterfall where people sometimes pass. In the end I decided it was lunchtime and I ate my sandwiches. When I had been sitting next to the water-fall for some time I began to wish it would stop because the noise went on and on and on, the same all the time, worse than the noise of the wheels of a train when you're travelling. I could hear nothing else; no noises came from the village which was only just over the brink of the crag under which I was sitting. The endless boom of water falling and echoing, the dank chill and utter loneliness began to oppress my spirits. I wished Camouflage was there. I finished painting my picture and packed up my things. Time must be getting on now, I thought; I'll go home to tea. As I walked up the little zig-zagging footpath to the village the noise of the waterfall receded. Suddenly there were birds chirrupping, wind in the treetops, the bus which had stopped momentarily in the village to pick up passengers outside the Fox and Hounds, its engine still running, cries of greeting, the crash of gears and the labouring of the engine as it started up the hill again. All this I could hear although it was still out of sight and it was such a relief, like coming out of the dryer at the hairdresser. I've only ever been once under one of those things and I promise when I grow up nothing will induce me to have my hair 'done' and waste all those hours sitting under that machine feeling as if I am never going to hear things naturally again.

When I came up into the sunlight on the village green the bus was gone; someone who had been met off it was being shepherded across the grass by a group of friends or relations carrying cases and talking eagerly, but otherwise there was no activity, no sign that anything had happened. An old man was sitting on the bench outside the Fox and Hounds. A cat rubbed herself against his legs. I wished I had Camouflage with me. But the most disappointing thing was the time: it was five past one. Really, I thought I had been working all day long, and now there was the whole afternoon to get through and nothing left to do. Because I wasn't going up to Bowden Farm. It was very tempting. I could just have got on my bicycle and ridden there in a few minutes and then Michael and I could have gone for a walk, but because I was alone I was not allowed to go up on the fell. I tried to think of things to do. I rode a little way along the main road that goes to Kettle-side and over into Wensleydale, the way the bus had gone, but there didn't seem much point; I would just have to ride back again once I got wherever I went. The afternoon was empty and useless. I thought again about going up to Bowden Farm, but instead I turned my back on it and rode back into Knares-ley and spent the rest of the day reading at Mrs Renton's, while my mother kept on telling me it was a pity to be indoors on a nice day like this and in the end we went out for a walk together, down by the cathedral.

The next morning I woke up feeling very gloomy. It was the day of the great concert. The sun was shining, the clouds were blowing across the sky, and I was doomed to do nothing. My mother was trying to get rid of me. 'Shall I make some sandwiches?' she said. 'What are you going to do?'

'I dunno.'

'What about Michael?'

'He's going to this concert.'

I kicked my heels for a little while longer. 'I wish I had Camouflage,' I said.

'Why not go and see her?' said my mother. 'They're not starting for Leeds until after lunch.'

I still sat around. Then at last I decided to stop being obstinate. It was so stupid when the only person who suffered was myself. My mother asked where I was going. Then she did a thing which is typical of my mother. Having been the first to suggest that I should visit Miss Barnaby, she now insisted I would be making a nuisance of myself and that Miss Barnaby was sure to be too busy because of the concert and so on and so on. Of course this made me all the more determined to go – (it suddenly occurs to me that I am very like my mother really. I only need a bit of opposition to make me quite pigheaded) so I agreed to do some shopping for my mother so as to get myself safely out of the house.

Of course my mother was wrong about Miss Barnaby. Nobody but my mother would be in a nervous twit for the whole morning simply because she was going to Leeds to a concert in the afternoon. Miss Barnaby was sitting reading when I arrived. 'I thought I would give my legs a bit of a rest,' she said as she rearranged them on the footstool, 'ready for our excursion. So come in and tell me all about your visit to your friends.'

'It was miserable,' I said. 'It's not worth talking about.'

'So you can now put behind you for ever any secret hankering you may have had to go back to Horsepath.'

'Oh, I didn't have any hankering anyway.'

'And yet I gather you were disappointed when you found your old house was for sale.'

I was surprised. I hadn't said anything about being disappointed. 'How did you know?' I asked.

She shrugged her shoulders. 'Perhaps you sounded disappointed. But you were, weren't you? – Even after being so sure you didn't want to go back there.'

'Yes,' I said. 'Nobody told me it was for sale. I was just walking down the road, feeling quite cheerful at that moment, as it happens; and there it was and I felt miserable, just as if a cloud had gone over the sun.'

'Nobody had told you it was for sale,' she repeated. 'Was it just a case of "Nobody ever tells me anything"? You were miserable because you felt aggrieved, unconsulted, uninformed?'

'Partly that. But it wasn't only that. I just hadn't believed in it till then – I mean, that we wouldn't go back, and Daddy and everything. Since Daddy turned up that time I've always been expecting something to *happen*. And, do you know? – Mummy spent that week I was away with Daddy in London. And I found out that it wasn't Sally that invited me but my mother that asked her mother to have me.'

'They had lots of things to discuss. Very grown-up things,' she said. 'They had to find out if they wanted to live together again. That's a difficult thing to decide when there's someone else there all the time.'

'You think that's what they did it for?' I asked. 'And which way do you think they decided?'

'I've not got second sight, you know! What did your mother say?'

'She said she didn't want to go back to Horsepath. She said

she was glad I liked Knaresley because she liked Knaresley too, and it would be perfect if we had a little house of our own. And Daddy has a landlady who spoils him, not like Mrs Renton, she said.'

'So you think it sounds as if they decided against it.' Miss Barnaby sat thinking for some time and then she said, 'I don't know. You'll only know the answer if you ask her yourself.'

'But she'll only snap my head off. And I'm so afraid of putting her against Daddy by sounding keen to go back to him. If I asked her she could just tell me a lie again, like she did before.'

Miss Barnaby sat stroking her chin. 'There's another thing you could do,' she said. 'Write to your father. Now that your mother has talked about him again and he's given you another present, it's only natural for you to want to write to him. Just say boldly to your mother, "I ought to write and thank Daddy. What is his address?" She could hardly take exception to that.'

It was an excellent idea. Knowing Mummy, she might even take it into her head to be cross if I didn't. 'That's what I'll do,' I said.

15

A gentleman from Leeds

Miss Barnaby let me take Camouflage out with me, and she gave me the key of the back door so that I could bring her home in the evening, because they wouldn't be back until late. 'You can give her her supper,' she said. 'Then she can't complain that I am neglecting her. I am always afraid that she is going to write to the R.S.P.C.A. That's why I'm so glad you take an interest in her. When she's a bit older she'll probably settle down, but at the moment she does demand such a lot of entertainment.'

I said I hoped she would never settle down to be quite such a stodgy character as Byron. Poor old Byron! Camouflage was scarcely a year old, and I expected him in his dotage to gambol around like her.

'Perhaps she'll have a family this summer,' said Miss Barnaby, 'and suddenly become a responsible matron.'

Camouflage, who was making a racket inside the basket seemed determined to remain as young and irresponsible as ever. So I went off as quickly as possible, not to keep her cooped up too long, had some difficulty with my mother who wanted to detain me with a long lecture about not imposing myself on people who were old and probably wanted a bit of peace – it was no good telling her Miss Barnaby was pleased to see me – but finally managed to extricate myself and set off for the dale with my sandwiches and Camouflage on the carrier. I had quite forgotten about feeling aggrieved about not going to the concert and when I met Michael, who was coming down on his bicycle to see how I was and said apologetically that he wished I were coming too, I said, (and I meant it), 'But I wouldn't enjoy it.'

'You know, it's a very special occasion for Miss Barnaby,' I said. 'And it's no good pretending I'm musical.'

'What are you going to do now?' asked Michael. Camouflage who had been quiet as long as she felt we were going somewhere, had begun to protest. 'The way humans expect one to sit cramped in a basket on the back of a bicycle while they have a long discussion about I know not what is insupportable,' she said, heaving about so much that she almost upset the bicycle.

'I was going to do a painting,' I said. I had not decided where.

'Let's go up to Fell Cottage,' Michael suggested. 'Then we can let Camouflage out. I shall have to go home soon. I promised my mother. She's afraid I'll set off for Leeds without brushing my hair or something.'

I thought it was a splendid idea to go up to Fell Cottage

because I remembered I had always intended to do a view of it from above where you can almost look down the chimney pots. I did not think it would qualify as going up on the fell if I just went up the road as far as that. We let Camouflage out, and about time too, she said, with indignant scrabbling and miaows as we unstrapped the basket, but as soon as we had raised the lid she decided to assert her independence by staying inside it. Michael and I went into the house, to Camouflage's great indignation as she expected her courtiers to remain at her beck and call until she deigned to leave her basket. When our eyes had got used to the dimness of the shuttered interior, I noticed one or two things were different. A large piece of wallpaper had been pulled away from the wall in the sitting-room and flapped in the draught. I decided this had not happened by accident or natural causes because we found an empty cigarette packet on the mantelpiece. After that we examined the whole place like a couple of detectives and found several cigarette ends but apart from that no undoubted signs of occupation, though I thought certain cupboards had not been standing open before and upstairs some more wallpaper had been pulled away, but I wasn't absolutely certain it hadn't been like that before.

'It's a pity it should be left to fall to pieces, any old tramp coming in, and next time they won't be satisfied with pulling paper down, they'll tear the cupboards out to make a fire,' I said. 'And it could be such a nice house to live in.'

'People don't want to live in remote spots like this,' said Michael, 'though I suppose someone might want it for a holiday cottage.'

After Michael had gone I settled down to do my picture. There was an excellent viewpoint on the road just above the cottage where I could see the roofs sloping at different angles, and chimney pots, with the bend of the road going round the house and the trees sheltering it from the wind. They were mostly ash trees and showed no sign of the spring, their buds still black and lifeless. I wished they were covered with leaves, as when I had first seen them, because it was going to be very difficult to paint all the branches and twigs, especially as through the branches and twigs I could see the dale, the line of trees along where Bowden Beck ran, and the fell opposite, all patchworked out with drystone walls and another road winding up over the top. There was such a lot to put in and it was so difficult to make some things look far away and others near at hand that when I had finished it looked a real mess. I was just wondering how I could have done it better when I heard a great shindy behind me. Camouflage was wedged half-way up a hawthorn tree, spitting and bristling, and a collie dog was running back and forth at the foot of it barking his head off. I looked around frantically to see if the dog had an owner anywhere at hand and was relieved to see an old man with a stick descending the road above me. At that moment his attention was caught by the excited barking of his dog and he began to call him. The dog retired discomforted at having to lose face before a cat but heeding the stern call of duty. I went to Camouflage's aid, as in her terror she seemed to have forced herself into a position from which she could not now extricate herself. There is nothing like a thorn bush for being inextricable. I had just got her out and was comforting her when she shot out of my arms into the bush once more. The old man, with his dog walking obediently to heel, had reached us.

'Hullo, Miss,' he said and then, perceiving Camouflage, 'Oh, it's that cat o' yours. I wondered what old Rover was on about. It's only t' little lass's cat. What a to-do! Hush, now! That's more like it, down! He wouldn't harm her – it's only because she takes fright and makes off that he gets moithered, don't you, Rover? There's a good dog! He gets on a treat with our Tabitha, don't you then? It's nobbut another pussy like our Tabby – but she's a rum-looking cat, now isn't she, more like a rabbit and such girt ears, for a cat, I reckon. I never saw owt like that afore.'

'She comes from Abyssinia,' I told him.

'Oh, ay, a foreigner, I might have guessed as much. Well there's no call, young puss, to take fright at poor old Rover. There never was a fonder dog. He'd make friends wi't' devil hisseln.' At the approach of the old man Camouflage arched her back and spat, determined to defend her stronghold in the thorn bush against all comers.

'Nay, nay, I wasn't doing owt to hurt you,' he said, withdrawing his hand quickly and sucking the blood from a scratch, though I don't know if it was a thorn or Camouflage who had done it.

'But haven't I seen you afore?' he said to me. 'You and your cat, weren't you with that young lad of Metcalfe's t' other day up on t' fell?'

Now that he mentioned it I remembered that it had been he, with a younger man and two dogs, one of them Rover, who had been driving a herd of cattle and a very irate bull along No Road for Motors on one occasion when we had been going up to Bowden Farm across the shoulder. He asked me if I came from round there, and I explained that I lived in Knaresley. Then he caught sight of my painting which I had left propped up against a stone at the roadside.

'Eh, you've never done this yourself?' he asked in the stupid way people always have – I mean who would bring a painted picture, paints and all the paraphernalia along and set them up in some lonely spot and wait for the next passer-by, if he or she were not actually engaged in painting the picture! So I told him that I was indeed painting the picture and he told me how clever it was and then asked, 'Is it anywhere about here?'

I ask you! It wasn't such a bad painting as all that and there he was staring at the cottage and staring at my picture of the cottage and saying, 'Is it anywhere about here?'

'It's meant to be Fell Cottage,' I said in suitably humble tones, 'I'm afraid it's not very like,' pointing out the cottage from where we stood, and he looked at it in surprise as if he had never noticed it could be seen from there.

'If you'd nobbut put in t' front door wi' t' little porch and that old Albertine rose climbing over it,' he said by way of apology, 'then I'd have kenned it straight off.'

I forbore to point out that the front door and porch could not be seen from this angle. Some people are quite blind.

He still tried to make up for failing to recognise my picture by telling me how pretty it was and how clever it was and how he didn't know how I could do it, he never could have done it, etc., and having at length exhausted this subject he turned to the subject of Fell Cottage itself.

'It's a right shame it's stood empty for so long,' he said. 'It used to be a real champion spot when old Mrs Ward lived there. She used to keep t' garden crammed full o' flowers. You couldn't beat that sunny little corner for growing things–it looked a right bobby dazzler! Ay, well, it's all tangled up wi' weeds now, you'd never believe how grand it used to look.'

'It's a great pity it should stand empty,' I said, 'because the longer it stands empty the more ramshackle and tumble-down it is going to look, and no one will want to live in it.'

'Ay, that's just it,' he said. 'My Missus, now, she keeps t' key, so she can show it to anyone that wants to come and buy t' place. Since last backend not a soul has been. Then before Easter there was a gentleman came from Leeds wanted to see over it. Very struck with it he was, and came again another time and brought another gentleman from t' city, artichoke, he said he was or something like – my missus will tell you, she's more of a scholar than I am – anyway, this arty chap went round wi' a measuring rod, he did, tapping everything and he looked at t' roof, and rived t' paper off t' wall. It fair upset her, my Missus said, to see the way he treated that nice paper, and Mrs Ward nobbut had it put on two years afore she died, but he wanted to see if it were damp behind. And he seemed to think it was pretty bad, but it's like you said, when a place isn't lived in, it gets damp in no time.'

'So they decided not to buy it?' I interrupted him, not knowing whether to be sorry or glad. I did not like the idea of city people smartening it up for a summer cottage (and, of course, we wouldn't be able to go there any longer). But on the other hand it would be a great pity if it fell into ruins altogether.

'Nay, they wouldn't tell t' likes of us. They'd only tell t' agent, them in Knaresley, that's trying to sell it for Mrs Ward's niece. Only my missus said she didn't think folks like that would ever want to live in such a lonely spot, though they did talk of putting in t' electricity, and all these new fangled contraptions like heating that you have under t 'floors and I don't know what else.'

'Perhaps they just wanted it for weekends and holidays,' I said.

'Yes, happen you're right,' he said struck by the idea. 'Ay, mebbe with summer coming we'll see more of these holiday makers from t' big towns, and I daresay one of them will come round to buy it. That's what happens to most of t' old cottages these days.'

That evening after tea I screwed up my courage to ask my mother for my father's address.

'Yes, you ought to write to him,' she said. 'I'm just writing to him myself so if you give me the letter I can put it in the same envelope. It'll save a stamp.'

I don't think she meant not to give me the address on purpose. She just meant what she said – it would save the stamp. But the result was I didn't dare write all I wanted to write because she would see it. I told him I was sorry I hadn't looked pleased to see him when he came; and I said I hoped I would see him again. But the rest of the letter was just about the places we had been to with the map. In the end I don't think Mummy did read the letter because I saw her put it straight into the envelope and seal it up. I hoped she would give it to me to post, but she didn't. I don't think that was on purpose, but perhaps it was.

16

Rabbit hunt

As April went on, the country began to change. In Horsepath I never noticed the spring much, but in the country it made all the difference in the world. It was the trees I noticed most. You never look at trees in a town; you see the daffodils coming out in people's gardens and you say spring is here at last and by the time it's summer the trees have got their leaves on them and that is that. At least, it was like that for me. Do you know I never even noticed that elm trees had flowers until I saw the big elms in the meadow below the cathedral all covered in bloom?

Further up the dale there are no elms. Everything is different up there. Only certain trees grow, ashes mostly, and sycamores along the beck just above Grewelthwaite, and larches in some places. There is a little wood of larches below one of the highest parts of No Road for Motors, where the ground drops away almost as steeply as a cliff and you'd scarcely think trees would find a foothold there, but they've grown very tall and strong.

Spring started much later up the dale. It's not very many miles from Knaresley but it's up hill all the way and the part through Hackfall woods is so steep that even Michael and I get off our bikes and walk. It's the height makes the big difference and means that sometimes the trees are a full fortnight later coming into leaf than they are in Knaresley. Even Hackfall woods, which are mostly beeches, had a start on the dale itself and the brown was hazed over with green before there was a sign of colour higher up. Then the big pink buds of the sycamores along the beck began to burst and the waxen, brownish fingers of leaf unclenched and began to spread themselves out in the light and go green. The larches were soon misted over with a vivid orangey green. But it was not until well into May that the black buds of the ash began to show any sign of life.

It was when the ashes were already sprouting a little pale green leaf in the second half of May, that I spent a weekend at Bowden Farm. I think Mrs Metcalfe thought I had been rather left out over the concert outing and although Michael would not let her say a thing against Miss Barnaby, he could not convince her that I was not musical. Anyway, it seemed to worry her for a long time and she used to say to me, 'We must think of something *special* for you.' That was how she came to ask me to stay for the weekend.

'Of course, it's nothing out of the way, not like going to Leeds for a concert and that marvellous young lady that plays the 'cello so wonderfully – Michael's always telling me her name but I can never remember it. But I thought mebbe you might just like to come up here for the weekend, so that you didn't have to think of going home before it gets dark. You could always bring Camouflage with you if Miss Barnaby didn't mind. Tigger needs some help catching the young rabbits at this time of year.'

She didn't know I'd rather have spent the night at Bowden Farm than gone to a dozen concerts and she would never have believed it, because Bowden Farm was so ordinary to her.

'You'll find it very quiet up here on a night,' she said to me on Friday night when she took me up to my bedroom. 'I'm glad you've got Camouflage to keep you company, because I know some city folks find it a bit creepy. We're used to it, and I couldn't abide the noise you get in towns.'

My room was quite small, with a sloping ceiling and a little window with a wide window-sill because the walls were so thick. Below the window, roofs of various sheds and out-houses sloped down almost to the ground which was very convenient for Camouflage because she could leave at her own convenience. There was a marble-topped washstand in my room and a big jug of water and a basin with roses on, because, as I discovered to my surprise, they had no bathroom. 'Do you never have a bath?' I asked Michael.

'Of course I have a bath,' he said, offended, 'in the peggy tub.'

I must say he always looked very clean, and never smelt or anything, like some of the children at school.

Also the only lavatory they had was in the yard. Mrs Metcalfe pointed out there was a chamber pot (with matching roses) under the bed, 'because you won't want to be venturing up the yard after dark,' she said. Of this I was very glad. Not that I am frightened of the dark and Bowden Farm was not spooky at all; but it was very cosy in my little room and a long long way to the bog (as Michael calls it).

I curled up in bed and when it had stopped plonging and rattling (it was an iron bedstead with a sort of springy metal net to sleep on) the silence of the night closed in round me. Actually it wasn't silent; I don't know how to explain it, but there are some sounds which seem to intensify the quiet and stillness, which one might not notice apart from them – such as the perpetual noise of water, the chuckling and rippling of Bowden Beck. Then there was the occasional baaing of sheep sounding far far away which gave a feeling of the emptiness and loneliness of the dale. One thing which frightened me at first was the cry of the owl, but what startled me most, and Camouflage too, was a shriek of pain; I'm sure it was pain. I went to the window, and so did she, bristling all over, and we looked out into the darkness, but all was still; nothing replied. Camouflage, who had been all alertness, every whisker tensed, suddenly discovered a pressing need to wash her left thigh. It really is a very good way to cover up a change in tactics. I climbed back into bed, and presently she followed me and curled up and settled down, though once or twice she raised her head and pricked her ears at distant cries.

In the morning when I woke she had already gone. 'I reckon she wanted to do a bit of night hunting herself,' Mrs Metcalfe remarked. I asked her what that shriek could have been, and she said some wild animal that had been caught by the owl, most likely. They seemed to take it so lightly, the Metcalfes, while that piteous cry still sounded in my ears. 'Nay, love, that's nowt to upset yourself over,' said Mrs Metcalfe. 'It's only nature. The old owl has to fend for himself, and we are glad of him, because he catches vermin that we want rid of. It's the same with your Camouflage. It's natural to all the beasts to kill and be killed.'

She had only just finished talking when Michael, who was in

the yard, called out 'Look out, you two! Here's Camouflage! She's caught summat.'

I ran out into the yard. Camouflage was approaching slowly because what she had in her mouth was almost as large as herself. She was half dragging it along the ground, stopping every few paces to get a better hold, or for a breather. At one such moment her victim, which she had left free on the ground before her, gathered his limbs together, flattened his ears against his back (I saw then that it was a young rabbit – such a sweet creature) and looked warily around to see if he had a chance to make off. Camouflage batted him one, and crouched back to see the effect of her blow. He was too dazed to know what to do.

I suddenly found my tongue and cried out, 'It's alive.' I suppose I expected everyone to rush to the rescue of the rabbit. I started to run towards Camouflage but quick as anything she picked up her rabbit and ran, awkwardly, but much faster than I expected, skirting the farmyard, looking for some cover where she could take refuge with her prey, and kill and devour him at her leisure. Nobody else moved to stop her. Even so, I almost caught her when she thought she could leap up on to a roof, forgetting how heavy and cumbersome the rabbit was. I had my hands on her for a moment, but leaving go of the rabbit she turned her head to snarl and hiss at me, writhing and lashing out at me with her claws. The rabbit took a step or two and if he had had any sense he could have got away then; but he evidently didn't know what was the best thing to do and Camouflage had wriggled free and caught him again before he had time to assemble his thoughts. This time she dragged him under a pile of timber where she was entirely unapproachable.

I don't think I was crying. I was just very horrified. I looked

round at everyone who had been standing watching this scene –
it had only taken a few seconds – and suddenly I realised that
they all thought it was very funny that I should want to save
the rabbit's life. Mr Metcalfe laughed outright and his wife was
smiling too though she said to him, 'Now then, I don't like to
see a little animal frightened out of its life myself either. Cats are
cruel the way they don't kill them straight off. If you just
shifted a bit of that timber there you could finish the poor
creature off. Come inside,' she said to me. 'Leave it to Michael's
Dad. He's got a soft heart underneath.'

I went into the kitchen because I didn't want to see what happened and then I went to the window because I couldn't bear
not seeing it. Michael was helping his father shift some of the
timber. Mrs Metcalfe enticed me away from the window.
'Come and sit over here, love,' she said. 'They won't be long.
And don't be vexed with poor Camouflage. She's likely very
proud of herself, and was fetching it home alive specially to
show you what she'd caught. Tigger catches any amount of
rabbits this time of year and Dad's always set up with him
because the rabbits are such a nuisance. We'd never grow anything in the garden if they had their own way. But I'm like you
– I hate to see it happen. Rabbits look so innocent when they're
young.'

There was a great scuffle in the yard. I rose from my seat, but
Mrs Metcalfe pushed me down again. 'They won't be long
now,' she said. And a moment later, Michael came in. 'We
got it,' he said triumphantly. 'It's a whopper. Camouflage is
right mad.'

'Is it dead?' I asked.

'Yes, Dad killed it. Just one clout behind the ears. It never
felt a thing.'

I started to cry. Poor little rabbit. Michael began to explain how it would have died instantly, hit in that particular place.

'Stop it, stop it!' I shouted. 'I don't want to hear.'

At last they left me alone. I wandered miserably around the farm. I hated Camouflage. She had spoilt everything. And now I had shouted at everyone else and I didn't know how I was going to say sorry. Perhaps I had better go home, and yet it was such a lovely day; the sun was shining, the wind was blowing, the fields were yellow with buttercups, the ashes were already beginning to look greener, and the larks were singing up in the sky. I lay down by the beck.

When I had been watching the movement of the brown water for some time, Camouflage appeared. She was chasing a butterfly and took no notice of me. Butterflies are more difficult to catch than young rabbits because Camouflage can't fly. The butterfly settled on some cuckoo flowers. Camouflage flattened her body to the ground and crept very very cautiously through the grass. The butterfly, quite unaware of its pursuer, moved on to another flower. Camouflage changed course and continued her stealthy progress. The butterfly, thinking of other things, flew up into the air just over Camouflage's head and she rose suddenly in a leap, almost falling over backwards as her outstretched paw hit nothing but air. The butterfly pursued its carefree way to other flowers in other fields while Camouflage found another butterfly to track down. I decided that I didn't hate her after all. Presently Michael turned up with a great parcel of sandwiches and a bottle of orange juice and we set out for a long day's outing with Camouflage at our heels, all as cheerful as could be.

17

Moonlight on the Fells

On Sunday night, the last night I was at Bowden Farm, Michael and I planned to have a midnight expedition because the moon was almost full and very bright. On Saturday night I had looked out of my bedroom window.

'Everything was so clear and bright and silvery,' I told Michael, 'That I wished I could slip out and walk down as far as the stepping-stones to see it all by the light of the moon.'

'Well, why didn't you?' he asked. 'Were you scared?'

'Oh, no,' I said, 'I'd have taken Camouflage. But your parents might be angry. I don't want them to be cross with me.'

'I tell you what,' said Michael, 'if it's another clear night tonight, we'll go together.'

'But what would your parents think?' I asked.

'They won't object if they only find out about it afterwards. It's like a midnight feast,' he said.

Mentioning feasts made us think we ought to take some food with us because it would make the expedition more of an event. We got some sandwiches with chocolate spread and some rock buns to take out with us on Sunday afternoon but instead of eating them we hid them down by the stepping-stones in a hole in the tree where I had first seen Michael. They were fastened up in a polythene bag so that they would not get damp in the dew.

'Now it probably won't be bright and clear tonight,' I said, 'then what shall we do?'

'We'll see,' said Michael.

About tea time it began to cloud over. There had been a few clouds before this, blowing across the sky, but now the clouds began to thicken up, rank upon rank, with here and there a shaft of sunlight falling upon some distant feature of the land-scape but no blue of the sky visible. Being the end of May it did not get dark until nearly ten o'clock, but the cloudy sky became more and more settled looking and we sat indoors and played games until it was time to go to bed. I felt rather gloomy because it was school tomorrow, and back home to Mrs Renton's after that. And I could not help thinking of the chocolate spread sandwiches and the rock cakes which I should have dearly liked to eat that afternoon and which were now uselessly marooned in the hole in the tree where we would scarcely be going to retrieve them. And so I went to bed sadly thinking how everything one enjoys always comes to an end and one can never enjoy the last part of it because one is thinking it is going to end soon. This thought seemed so profound and true that I even brought tears to my eyes. But it didn't seem worth crying so I lay listening to the wind, which had dropped earlier at about the time of sunset but had now risen again. And so I fell asleep.

I awoke suddenly. I had the feeling something had awakened me and I raised myself on one elbow so that my head was clear of the pillow, and listened. Moonlight was streaming in through the window but my brain was still so clogged with sleep that I did not remember that moonlight had any importance. Then I heard the sound of Michael's door being gently closed and I suddenly thought 'Oh! Our midnight walk! Our midnight feast!'

The wind, to which I had been listening before I went to sleep, had been working hard ever since clearing the clouds out of the sky. It was still blowing now, but there was not a cloud left in sight. Michael came into my room, already dressed.

'Want to come after all?' he whispered.

Actually I felt so warm and comfy in bed that I would almost rather not have got up, but I remembered hard how much I had been looking forward to this, and how, as soon as we had started off, I would enjoy it. So I put on my clothes, and we all three, including Camouflage, set off, quietly, quietly, down the stairs and out into the yard.

The moon was very high in the sky, the wind was blowing and everything was very, very clear, much clearer and sharper than it had been during the day. There was no mist, nor anything in the atmosphere to dim or blur what was far away, but this did not make the dale seem any smaller nor the far fells any nearer. They just looked more naked, and lonely and empty, and so unlike the familiar places where I had walked or climbed that I could not imagine it was possible to walk there. I think it was this that made the dale seem almost bigger than by familiar daylight.

It is very curious the effect of brightness there is with moonlight, although it is actually much darker than ever it is by daylight. I think it is because the shadows are so dark and black and bottomless, and the edge between the shadow and the light is as sharp and sudden as if it had been cut with scissors. An old ash, half-way up the fell opposite the stepping-stones, which was very backward with not much leaf showing, cast a net of shadow across the rock face which rose almost vertically behind it; the funny thing was that the shadow was more real than the tree itself, which I could only make out with great difficulty while from where we stood, which was at least half a mile away, we could see the black shadow upon the brightness of the hillside, with all the intricate shapes cast by the bare branches of the tree.

I don't want to go on for ever describing things, but I want to give you some idea of what it was like, how bright it was and how dark it was and also how empty it seemed at first. But to Camouflage the night was not empty and soon I began to notice the tiny squeakings and patterings and rustlings which I could hear if I stood very still under the trees by the beck, on the strip of land where the grass grew long because it was not enclosed with a dry-stone wall to turn it into a proper field. This was where the footpath went that followed the river and led from the stepping-stones to Bowden Farm.

Camouflage was torn between her desires as a huntress and her delight in human company on a walk at this hour. Some minute noise would catch her attention and she would tense her every muscle, her ears pricked, watching, listening; but at another moment she would go utterly moonstruck and mad, caper around and, racing ahead, disappear into the yawning mouths of shadows, only to leap out upon us as we passed by. I caught her mood and began racing and dancing along with her, and when, in the midst of one mad race, I suddenly stopped short to listen, she stopped as suddenly and, certain that I had seen or sensed some enemy lurking, snarled at the darkness ahead of us, bristling her bottlebrush tail. I laughed and told her there was nothing there, but she did not believe me and spat violently at a tree stump which fluttered a leaf at her, and advanced very gingerly in her prowling position, body lowered, fur on end. Her terror was catching and I began to fancy nameless monsters in the shadows and went back to Michael, who was following more sedately, and insisted on holding his hand.

I was relieved when we emerged on to the smooth moonlit stretch of grass by the stepping-stones. I immediately went mad again and started turning somersaults; Camouflage went mad too and from an ambush in the bushes she would make sudden sallies into the moonlight to attack me, retiring rapidly to cover when I tried to catch her. No one would have thought she was a tame animal at these moments; she had worked herself up into such a wild mood, launching into vicious attacks and then fleeing as if her life depended upon it. One time I chased her, flapping my arms, and she fled across the stepping-stones. Half-way across she found herself no longer pursued, paused and decided to catch the cheeky water which wouldn't stay still but formed a running noisy arch around the stone she stood on. At least, she may actually have been trying to catch fish, but I think she was just playing at catching the beck, which spitefully paid her out by drenching her paw. Camouflage sat on her stepping-stone, shaking her wet paw and looking affronted.

Michael and I climbed into the tree to eat our chocolate spread sandwiches and the rock cakes and I began to grow calm. The water was endlessly running below us; otherwise it was very quiet and still.

'You're very lucky,' I said to Michael. 'I wish I lived out here, with nothing but the sound of the wind and the beck, instead of the shunting of trains and the roar of traffic we get on Station Road, and all this emptiness instead of people all over the place.'

'You won't go on living at Mrs Renton's for ever, will you?' he asked. 'Have they sold your house in Horsepath?'

'I dunno.'

'And the furniture, what happened to all the furniture?'

I shrugged my shoulders. I hadn't asked any more questions. My father had written me a little note, enclosed in a letter to my mother, but all he said was that he was glad I liked Knaresley and he hoped he would see me some day soon. Nothing more specific than that.

'Mummy talked about having a little house of our own in Knaresley,' I said to Michael. 'Perhaps we'll have some of the furniture for that. But I don't know when that's going to be.'

We walked back to Bowden Farm much more quietly than we had come. Camouflage disappeared half-way home but we did not worry too much about her. She could look after herself. Clouds were coming up over the sky and from time to time they covered the face of the moon. There were cows coughing and sighing in the fields and a dog barked when we entered the farmyard, and then, finding it had made a mistake, was silent. As we crept up the stairs I heard Mrs Metcalfe say to Mr Metcalfe, 'It's only those bairns. They've been up to some mischief in the moonlight. Leave them be.'

18

Accident

In June Mrs Renton went to stay with her daughter and my mother said, 'What a relief to have her out of the house! How marvellous to feel that I can walk in at the front door and know that she will not open her sitting-room door and say, "Mrs Wintersgill, do you think I could have a word with you?" and then in her peevish long-suffering way ask if I could possibly try to shut the bathroom door a little more quietly if I happen to go in there after eight in the evening because she does suffer so with her ears – she used to find it such a trial when Mr Renton was alive, he used to play that 'cello of his, it did give her such a headache, and, besides, the ceiling has never been the same since we got so much traffic on Station Road – it is wicked the way the heavy lorries have been diverted along here to avoid going over the old bridge – and every time I shut the bathroom door she thinks the ceiling is going to fall on her head – and could I see that Miss Ruth wipes her feet when she comes in – and she's seen that cat round here again. This last is said as if I ought immediately to be struck with guilt on hearing "that cat" mentioned, so I look all innocent and say "what cat?" At which she draws in her breath sharply and says, "I won't have any cats in the house, and I tell everyone that when they come, Mrs Wintersgill." By the way, I *have* seen that cat around. Good thing Mrs Renton's away.'

'Camouflage?' I said. 'When? Where?'

'Oh, she was hanging about by the gate when I came home from school. She wanted to come into the house but I was firm with her. "Miss Barnaby will be wondering where you are," I said to her. "Run along home," I said. There's no point in encouraging her to come here even while Mrs Renton is away, because she won't know to stay away when she comes back.'

I looked out of the window, but she was not there now. 'All you care about is that cat,' said my mother, but she didn't look cross about it. Instead she put her arm round me affectionately and said, 'Some day we'll get out of this place and live in a little house of our own with roses round the door and a cat on the hearthrug and every modern convenience.'

'Have you sold the house in Horsepath?' I asked her.

'We've had an offer,' she said, 'at last! They want to turn it into flats, which would be a very good idea. It's quite uninhabitable as a single house. Anyway, they have to have their plans approved or something and that's what we're waiting for.'

I felt very nervous. I wanted to ask all sorts of questions– about Daddy, of course, and where we were going to live. Suppose I asked point-blank, 'Are we going to live with Daddy again?' But no, I was frightened she would be angry and say, 'Of course not. Whatever made you think that?' or something worse because she would think my asking that meant I didn't like living with her.

'Will there be enough money to buy a house in Knaresley, then?' I asked.

'I hope so,' said my mother. 'That's what you'd like, isn't it? When we first came here I never thought I'd want to stay. But now I actually like teaching at the Modern school and I feel it would be a pity to go somewhere else just when I'm beginning to make some headway with my pupils here. And you've settled down, too – at first you were so miserable that I wished I'd never come here and torn you away from all your little friends. But now we're both happy so why move again?'

She's decided she's happier without Daddy, I thought. Well, I had come to the same conclusion myself, but I still felt disappointed. I tried to comfort myself by thinking of the dale and Michael and Miss Barnaby and Camouflage. Meanwhile Mummy went on talking, almost to herself.

'I ought to have got a job long ago,' she said, 'and insisted on leaving that awful barrack. Then perhaps none of this need have happened. Oh well, all's well that ends well, I suppose, if it does end well. There are no happy endings in real life, you know, Ruth, only compromises. When one is young one thinks everything is going to be marvellous, but it doesn't turn out that way. In the end one finds oneself patching up a bad job and hoping for the best. It's a fresh start anyway. So long as you're happy . . .' she finished in a questioning tone.

'I'll be happy,' I said, swallowing a lump in my throat. Poor Mummy, she sounded so sad. I didn't know she cared so much about my being happy. And it was the first time she had ever said anything to suggest she thought it was partly her fault and not all Daddy's. When she was like this, talking to me as if I was a friend who could understand and not just a child to whom it was a nuisance to give information, I felt that at a pinch I could do without Daddy because Mummy needed someone to take care of her.

'Cheer up,' I said, patting her hand. 'We'll both be happy.'

'Of course, we will,' she said and blew her nose. Then in quite a different tone of voice she said, 'There's that cat of yours again.'

Camouflage had appeared on the window-sill.

'I told you she was around,' said my mother. At first she did not intend to let her in, but Camouflage sitting plaintively on the window-sill – it was still light so we did not want to draw the curtains – soon overcame her resistance. Camouflage made a great show of being ravenously hungry but my mother refused to give her anything to eat. At last she relented sufficiently to give her a saucer of milk.

'It's too late for you to go traipsing off to Palace Road,' she said. 'I'm putting her outside when we go to bed and if she's still here tomorrow morning you can take her back then.'

'But suppose Miss Barnaby gets worried?' I asked.

'She must know by now that the cat's likely to come running round here.'

'She hasn't been round here for ages,' I reminded my mother.

'Well, I'm not letting you go off to Palace Road now and that's that. Miss Barnaby should have a telephone if she wants to know the latest news of the whereabouts of her cat.'

So I had to go to bed and the next morning Camouflage was still there, sitting on Mrs Renton's doorstep. I gave her some breakfast when my mother wasn't looking and after breakfast I set off to Miss Barnaby's with Camouflage in the cat basket. I should have mentioned it was a Saturday, so I didn't have to go to school. I hadn't seen Miss Barnaby since the weekend before and I was longing to tell her the latest news about my parents. But no one answered the door. I pulled the bell lever again after a decent pause, and I could hear it clanging away in the kitchen regions so I knew it was working.

'Well,' I thought, after I had stood there another long age, 'I suppose she's gone out shopping.' I wondered what to do. I could let Camouflage out of the basket and leave her there, but the disadvantage of that was that she'd probably follow me. Or I could leave her in the basket, but then I didn't know how long Miss Barnaby was going to be out. She might be out all day for all I knew.

I opened the basket and let Camouflage out and she immediately ran to the front door and sat there beseeching me to let her in.

'No, Pussy dear,' I said, 'I haven't got the key. You wait there like a good pussy. Miss Barnaby may be back any minute.'

I went to my bicycle. Camouflage followed me incredulously with her eyes. I fastened on the basket and made to ride off. Camouflage came racing alongside me and I was frightened of hitting her because she will cut across my bows without any warning, so I flung down my bicycle and went back to the front door.

'Now, look, Pussy,' I said and then I suddenly had a good idea. There was a bottle of milk standing by the front door. I had seen it before, and moved it, because it was standing in the sun. 'I'll give Camouflage some milk,' I thought. 'That'll keep her occupied while I ride away.' I looked around for something to put it in. Of course I could always pour some on the step but Camouflage probably wouldn't clean it up very efficiently and then it would smell unless Miss Barnaby noticed it (very unlikely) and cleaned it up. So I stood there with the bottle in one hand and Camouflage milling round my feet asking for milk and to be let in. Then suddenly something struck me as rather odd.

'Which day of the week is it?' I said out loud and then answered myself, 'Saturday, of course, I'm not at school.' I usually went to Miss Barnaby's on a Saturday and I remember her saying more than once, 'It's such a nuisance, the milk doesn't come till after midday on a Saturday and there's never enough for breakfast for me and Camouflage. You see, on other days he comes before breakfast, but because he goes round collecting money on a Saturday he's much later. I ought to remember to ask for two pints on a Friday.'

It *was* a Saturday, wasn't it? I couldn't have made a mistake? I walked down the drive to the gate vaguely thinking I might see the milkman approaching or something, perhaps a neighbour whom I could ask about the milk delivery. There was no one in sight. I went back to the house and smelt the milk. It was sour.

Now, why hadn't Miss Barnaby yet taken yesterday's milk off her doorstep? For a moment I was cross with her – fancy going away and making no arrangements for Camouflage. But then, I thought, making excuses for her, perhaps she hadn't intended to go away. Perhaps she had just gone for the day somewhere and then decided to stay the night. That was why she hadn't cancelled the milk. But then, she must have been away two nights by now because the milk came before breakfast on Friday morning. She could always have rung me up from wherever she was and asked me to go round and feed Camouflage. But again, perhaps she had arranged for Camouflage. Perhaps she had asked one of the neighbours to feed her, but Camouflage had decided she would rather come round to see us. But then she must have forgotten to cancel the milk.

There was another alternative. Suppose Miss Barnaby was ill, too ill to come downstairs and fetch the milk? I know it's a preposterous idea, I thought, but suppose it's true. Nobody else but me is likely to call at the house and wonder why Miss Barnaby isn't there. If she were ill, having no telephone, she could lie there for days without anybody knowing.

My heart had begun to pound very hard. What was I going to do? I wished the milkman or somebody would turn up and it weren't all left to me. Should I go and find one of the neighbours (none of whom I knew)? I was rather frightened of looking a fool if there was some simpler explanation of the mystery of the sour milk so I decided to walk round the house and see if there was anywhere I could get in and then I could find out if Miss Barnaby was there or not.

Camouflage was still hanging around waiting to be let in, so I said to her, 'Come on, don't just sit mewing at that door. We can't get in there, that's certain. Can't you show me any other way in?'

We went round the house and I tried all the doors. The windows were all sash windows with latches in the middle which were all locked and anyway the bars on the outside are almost flush with the pane and give no purchase to the fingers, so I don't think I could have moved them even if they hadn't been locked. There was a window open upstairs but I didn't know how I could get at it, and apart from that there was only one window open which was the kitchen. The kitchen was on the ground floor from the inside, but outside the ground dropped away so that it was well out of my reach. The window was open about an inch at the bottom – room enough to slip my fingers in and lift the sash – which would make entry much easier than by the upstairs window which was open at the top. I looked around a bit, and found an outside lavatory with a step ladder in it. When I stood on the top of the ladder the window-sill came just below shoulder height. I opened the window. That was easy, but the next step was more difficult. The window-sill was covered with things, pots of jam, a milk bottle with a little milk in it, two teacups (Rockingham, of course) which hadn't been washed up, butter in a butter dish, a tin of cat food, opened and half empty and with maggots crawling in it, and a little dish of cold ham which she had covered with a cloth. I suppose the window-sill, with the window just that little bit open, was the coolest place in the kitchen for keeping milk, butter, and such like, while the teacups had got there because there was no other space available. One by one, I put the things down on to the floor inside which I could just reach if I pulled myself up on to the tips of my toes hanging onto the window frame with one hand while I moved the things with the other. It was a long job which was not made any easier by Camouflage, who had come up the ladder and was rubbing herself round my feet. I decided to put her through the window first so as to get her out of the way so I popped her on to the window-sill where she made herself a still further nuisance by standing expectantly mewing instead of jumping into the room. Eventually she jumped down on to the floor and I heaved myself up on to the window-sill, cleared a space on the floor and then stepped into the room.

I rather hoped Miss Barnaby would not walk into the kitchen at that moment because I would look such a fool, but a moment later I corrected my thoughts. It would be much better if she walked in, because it would be awful if she really were ill.

The mess in the kitchen was the same as usual. I had come so often that I had almost ceased to notice it. There was the smell too. It struck me with renewed force today – that smell of drains, of stale food, of cat, of damp and dust. Poor Miss Barnaby, I thought, if she is ill, whatever will become of her . . .

I resisted Camouflage's entreaties for food – she had turned up her nose at the flyblown tin – and went out into the hall at the foot of the stairs. My heart was going pit-a-pat. 'Miss Barnaby,' I called, 'Miss Barnaby!'

I stood in the dim gloomy hallway and listened and then I heard a sort of cough or gasp, faintly, from upstairs. I ran up. There on the landing was Miss Barnaby. I almost fell over her. She lay in a sort of crumpled heap; she had evidently fallen down the two or three steps which led from a room on the right. I knelt down beside her. She was trying to say something but I could not understand. No sound came – she only moved her lips. I leant closer and she tried again. The sound came suddenly, unexpectedly, and did not fit the word she was making with her lips but suddenly I understood, or guessed, that she was asking for water. I tried various doors, found the bathroom and brought her a tooth mug of water which I had to lift to her lips as she was too weak to do it herself. I was trying to think what I should do, what I should do first – all those things girl guides learn, but not being a girl guide I didn't know.

'I'll go for the doctor,' I said. She nodded her head just slightly. 'I won't be long,' I said, and I ran downstairs, unbolted the front door, remembered to leave it on the latch, leapt on my bicycle, and pedalled for all I was worth down to Dr Bradwell's.

19

A house of our own

Miss Barnaby had fallen down the two steps (there were only two of them) that led from her bedroom down to the landing, and because old people's bones are very brittle, so Dr Bradwell tells me, she had managed to break the thigh bone of her right leg. This must have happened on the Friday morning when she was coming down to breakfast. She had been quite unable to get up, and there was nobody's attention she could have attracted. Unfortunately, her old charlady did not come on Fridays. So she had lain there for twenty-four hours until I came and rang the doorbell, but even then she could not shout loud enough to attract my attention. Every time I thought how easily I could have gone away without suspecting anything, I felt like one does going down in a rather fast lift, my heart and stomach seemed to take a sudden dive. She could have lain there until she died of starvation.

While we were waiting for the ambulance I gave Camouflage, who was still demanding something to eat, a whole tin of
cat food which I found in a cupboard in the kitchen. I talked to
her and told her what a clever cat she was and how she had
saved Miss Barnaby's life, but she hadn't a clue what I was on
about, and hadn't taken the slightest interest in Miss Barnaby
since our entry into the house. However, she was very pleased
with the bumper breakfast and, since she had probably had
nothing the day before, she deserved it.

Dr Bradwell had gone next door to use the telephone and the
neighbour came back with him 'to see if there was anything
she could do'. I think she was just overcome with curiosity
because she peered into all the rooms, and she peered into the
kitchen while I was feeding Camouflage and said, 'Oh, I'm
sorry, I didn't know you were there,' and then she came in and
looked round.

'We never saw much of Miss Barnaby,' she said, 'she kept
herself to herself. Sometimes one never set eyes on her for days
on end.' It was the third time I'd heard her say that and she made
it sound almost like a complaint, as if someone was blaming her
for not having noticed that something had happened to Miss
Barnaby. I was very glad that the front door bell rang then, and
she did not go on talking to me.

It was, of course, the ambulance which had arrived. Dr
Bradwell had given Miss Barnaby something to stop the pain
and she was unconscious so I couldn't say goodbye. Before this
I had felt sort of noble and heroic but now I found I was crying
and I didn't want it to be noticed by the awful neighbour who
was telling someone that old ladies should not be allowed to
live by themselves, they ought to go into old people's homes.

At last the ambulance drove off and Dr Bradwell turned to
me and asked if he could give me a lift. (I had left my bicycle

at his house.) 'Who's going to look after the cat?' he said.

The neighbour hurried to explain that it wouldn't get on with her dog and he said he knew Mrs Renton wouldn't allow any animals in the house.

'She's away,' I said triumphantly. 'And after that she can go to a friend of mine where she's stayed before.'

'Good,' said Dr Bradwell, so as soon as we had locked up we left.

When I got home I was full of it all. I was going to tell my mother the whole story from beginning to end. Looking back it all seemed terribly exciting, like something out of a book, and I began to feel all noble and heroic again, and there was a lump in my throat. But as I went upstairs I heard voices coming from our front room. I didn't know whether to interrupt or not, so I let Camouflage out of her basket and hung around in the kitchen waiting for the visitor to go. I couldn't settle to doing anything else because I wanted to tell someone all about it, and then, I thought, I'll go up to Bowden Farm and tell Michael all about it.

Presently the door of the front room opened and my mother came out saying, 'I'll make some coffee. I can't think what's become of Ruth,' and then, seeing me, 'Why she's been here all the time,' and seeing Camouflage, 'I thought you were taking that cat back to Miss Barnaby's.'

I was just about to explain everything when my father came out of the front room and said, 'How's my little Ruth?' and gave me a hug.

Well, well! You could have knocked me over with a feather, specially after what Mummy had said the night before. But then, Daddy had written that he hoped he would see me soon. Still, she might have *told* me, if she was expecting him so soon.

Meanwhile my mother started saying, 'I thought you were going to take that cat round to Miss Barnaby's. Last night you thought she was going to be worried if you didn't take it round immediately and now we're just going out – we were only waiting for you because I thought you'd gone round there already.'

'I have gone round there already,' I said. 'Miss Barnaby's gone into hospital.'

'Well, what a good thing Mrs Renton's away,' said my mother and did not ask a word about what was wrong with Miss Barnaby. 'Do you want some coffee after all or shall we go straight away?' she asked my father.

'Let's go straight away,' he said.

'You can have the coffee if you want to.'

'No, let's go.'

'I only meant to say since we were going to have the coffee while we were waiting for Ruth, it doesn't seem worth having it now she's turned up.'

'You're quite right. Don't let's have any.'

'But you can certainly have some if you want.'

'I don't my dear, really I don't.'

'I don't want to make you feel . . . '

'I don't want any coffee. Don't you want to see this house?'

'Now don't start getting cross,' said my mother, getting up on her high horse. 'Of course I want to see the house.'

At the first mention of 'house' I pricked up my ears. So this wasn't just a visit to see us. Could Daddy be choosing a house for us to live in, just Mummy and me? Or . . . ? What other explanation could there be for 'the house'? With my mother momentarily incensed I decided to wait until events explained themselves.

She had recovered her good humour by the time we had got downstairs and climbed into my father's car. She patted his hand and said, 'Just like old times.'

Just like old times, I thought, they're arguing already. 'Isn't it fun?' she said, 'I'm so excited about this house!'

'Don't set your hopes too high,' he said. 'I got Arnold to come out and look it over and he was very pessimistic.'

'What on earth did you get Arnold to look at it for? He's an absolute fool. I could design a house better myself. Look at that one he did for the Thatchers . . .' and so she went on, demonstrating the stupidity of all architects and of Arnold in particular while my father drove on with a little smile upon his face. We were driving through Hackfall woods. The trees were now dark and heavy with leaf and inside the wood it was shady and mysterious. We drove on to Grewelthwaite and drew up outside a cottage.

'I must just pick up the key,' said my father and presently returned with some keys on a ring and got back in the car.

'Your friend Michael lives somewhere up here, doesn't he?' asked my mother.

I pointed out the road to Bowden Farm as we were going round the village green. We drove back along the road we had approached by.

'The turning is somewhere here,' said my father, slowing down. 'There's a little bridge.'

It's not, it couldn't be – but it was! We turned down No Road for Motors.

'It's rather an isolated position,' said my father, doubtfully.

My mother made no comment. We drew up outside Fell Cottage. 'Is this it?' she asked with obvious disappointment. My heart sank.

'It's been empty almost a year,' my father said apologetically. 'I told you it was in very dilapidated condition. We would want to gut it entirely.'

We. It could only mean, it must be . . . How stupid of me! I had never thought that Daddy could come and live with us in Knaresley, instead of us going to live with him in Horsepath. Mummy might have told me. But then perhaps she thought she had told me – she didn't know that I thought living in Knaresley equalled living without Daddy. If only she would like the house!

My mother looked up at the front of the house. I suppose it was the boarded windows that made it look so derelict. The Albertine rose was in bud but not yet out and it had never been cut or fastened back. Long trailers looped down and swung across the path. A rampant mixture of weeds and flowers filled the bed and overflowed on to the path. My mother snagged her stockings. Not a good start.

My father unlocked the front door and we went in. It felt odd entering by the door, and odd to see sunlight pouring in. At first we could see nothing and had to wait for our eyes to get used to the dark.

'Arnold thought you would want to take on something in rather better trim than this,' said my father in a small voice.

'What does that man think he knows about me and my tastes!' she snorted. Daddy winked at me behind her back. It was just as it had been – you had to say the opposite of what you wanted. I started to pretend to explore and opened the kitchen door. 'I suppose this must be the kitchen,' I said peering in; 'Very primitive,' (which is what my mother was always saying about the kitchen at 'that barrack'. 'The kitchen arrangements are primitive in the extreme,' she would say if anyone dared to say a word of praise for the house).

She and Daddy stood in the doorway and looked round the kitchen. 'I'm afraid it's rather small,' he said.

'I like a small kitchen,' said Mummy. 'You men have no idea what a kitchen should be like because you don't have to work in one. The miles I had to walk in that kitchen at Horsepath! And all because it was so badly planned. You don't want a vast great kitchen unless you've got an army of cooks, but you must have things in the right places, the sink next to the cooker – we could put it here,' she said, advancing into the room, 'and do away with that of course' (pointing at the range), 'but just look at all these marvellous cupboards!'

'And there's a larder here,' I said, opening the door.

'Ah, yes, there's such a lot of storage space, I don't know how you can say the kitchen's small. Of course, we would have to lay a new floor, these flags would be very hard on the feet.'

And so it went on from room to room. We had only to suggest that something was wrong for my mother to argue hotly that everything was right, and if anything was needed to tip the balance the dreaded name of Arnold only had to be mentioned.

'I can't think why he should imagine that damp is such a problem. As an architect he must know all the new methods that have been invented, like running a certain sort of electric current through the walls, and I believe that it's not very expensive and completely effective.'

So she planned where the bathroom would go and what sort of central heating we should have, but the thing that pleased her most of all was the cow shed at the end of the house. It was part of the same building and went up two storeys, and the huge doors at the end when opened wide gave a view right out towards the plain of York with Knaresley just visible where the last spur of the foothills descended to the plain.

She stood in the middle amongst the straw and the smell of old cow dung and drew a great sigh and said, 'What a marvellous room this would make! A great big window on this side for the view, and one over here to catch the sun, and think of all this height! My only complaint against the other rooms is that they are the tiniest bit too low. But if we have this room to stretch our necks in, that won't matter.'

When my father started talking about money, and how expensive it would be, she burst out indignantly, 'But I thought the whole point was that if we bought something very cheap like this, just as a shell, we could afford to spend as much again, or twice as much again, making it just how we wanted it. After all, you're getting a pretty good price for that barrack of a place in Horsepath.'

My father went on demurring and talking of expense and looking through some papers he had, and saying didn't she think she ought to look at this house on the Leeds Road in Knaresley before she made up her mind.

'That place!' exclaimed my mother, 'I know just what it's like, – gaunt, Victorian, miles of corridor and staircase. I'm not living in another house like that. Nor in a semi-detached horror like that,' she said snatching the papers from him and going through them one by one. 'Nor in this modern box with a view of a dozen other modern boxes, nor in this chalet bungalow – good heavens! What a load of rubbish you've got here!'

'It's only what the agent gave me,' he protested. 'I wasn't suggesting you should live in any of those.'

'Besides,' my mother went on, brushing him aside, 'this is where Ruth wants to live, she's absolutely mad about the country, aren't you, dear?'

'Yes,' I said in heartfelt tones.

'You see!' she exclaimed in triumph.

20

Conclusion

Daddy took us out to a posh lunch and Mummy talked the whole time about what she was going to do with Fell Cottage and how she was going to have a such-and-such like so-and-so but nothing would induce her to have a frightful thingummy like someone else. And then they fell to arguing about what furniture would go where and each swore that the other had quite forgotten how big this wardrobe was or how small that table. They got to the point of staring balefully across the table at one another and then Mummy started laughing and Daddy started laughing and they hugged one another and then they hugged me.

I told them how I had painted a picture of Fell Cottage. Mummy had seen the picture before and remembered it and said she wished I had taken her up behind the house and shown her where she could almost look down the chimney pots. I told them how the old man had told me about the gentleman from Leeds who had come to see the house together with an artichoke and Mummy thought it was a good joke and said Arnold had about as much brains as an artichoke. And I said Camouflage knew the house well already.

As soon as I mentioned Camouflage, I remembered about Miss Barnaby and so did Mummy.

'What was that you said about Miss Barnaby being ill?' she asked.

So I told them the whole story.

Mummy rang up the hospital for me to find out how she was and they said she was comfortable which sounded good, only Mummy says it is what they always say at hospitals and means nothing. They said she would not be well enough to have any visitors the next day and since Sunday is the only day they allow children under the age of fourteen to visit, it was a whole week before Michael and I were able to go and see her. The hospital was in Harrogate and Mrs Metcalfe drove us there. I was glad Mummy didn't come because I wanted to tell Miss Barnaby all about what had happened. Mrs Metcalfe came in with us but she was very shy; I almost think she was frightened of her. She sat right at the end of the bed and never said anything except, every now and then, 'Now, you mustn't tire Miss Barnaby with all your chatter.' To which Miss Barnaby replied, 'I'll let you know when I can bear no more.' In the end she said, 'I think perhaps you had better tell me the rest another time,' and Mrs Metcalfe took us away.

I was shocked at the way Miss Barnaby looked. I know she had always looked very old with her white wispy hair and her thin, parchment-coloured face with scarcely any teeth, but somehow she had always looked so full of life in her own house. Now she looked even paler lying against a heap of pillows, and in a nightdress and bedjacket one noticed much more those sinews (or whatever they are) which hang beneath the chin, and the veins, all blue and ropy, on her bony wrists and hands. Her cheeks looked more hollow than before and her mind seemed to wander, so that sometimes she did not seem to take in what I said. When we left she squeezed my hand and said, 'You must tell me all about it another time, when I am better.'

Soon after this she moved to a nursing home, also in

Harrogate, and when we went to visit her she was usually dressed and sitting on the terrace in a basket chair, but there still seemed to be something about her that looked older, as if the life had gone out of her. She could not play her 'cello because she could not sit properly. Her leg was still in plaster. Michael used to bring his violin and they allowed us to go into a special room in the nursing home where he could play for her. I think she liked this very much and I'm sure she liked our visits though the grown-ups thought perhaps she didn't.

'It's such a change to have a sensible conversation,' she used to say. 'No one here talks about anything but Bingo and television. And, of course, their operations.'

But when we said, 'When you come home,' she would say, 'No, I shall never be able to go back there and live by myself.' Then she looked defeated, as if she had lost a fight and did not care to go on living after it. And so I squeezed her hand and said, 'You must come and live with me when I'm grown up.' Mummy had told me that she would probably have to go and live in an old people's home and I knew she was sad about this because she is not gregarious and likes to walk by herself.

'I'm sure to live to be a hundred and six, so you'd better not make any rash promises,' she said. 'You give Camouflage a home instead and I'll be very grateful to you.'

Camouflage had stayed with us for a few days and then, before Mrs Renton came home, she went up to stay with Michael at Bowden Farm. Meanwhile Mummy and Daddy had decided to buy the house. Bit by bit I learnt what had happened and what was going to happen. Daddy had got a different job with the same firm which meant that he wouldn't be away from home all the time, but when he found that Mummy and I had settled down so happily in Knaresley he decided that it would be better if we all lived there and he travelled into Leeds every day. So he started to try to sell the house in Horsepath. Just before Easter he had come to see Fell Cottage, but since nobody else seemed to be in a hurry to buy it, he decided to wait until he had sold the other house.

I never knew it took so long to buy a house. Weeks and weeks went by while the solicitors were 'conveyancing' and term was over before 'completion'. And even then it seemed as if we were going to have to go on living at Mrs Renton's for months while the builders were in. But Daddy had a wonderful idea and he managed to persuade Mummy that it had been her idea in the first place; and so we hired a caravan and parked it outside Fell Cottage and we went and lived in it while the builders were at work. We almost didn't get it across the little bridge on to No Road for Motors but the old man and his missus who kept the key put rugs and mats over the stone parapet of the bridge and stood around and made helpful noises and it just got over. There really were only a few inches to spare but the rugs and mats prevented it from getting any scratches.

It really was a splendid idea, because not only did it mean that we could leave Mrs Renton's, but also that Mummy could keep an eye on the builders and see that they did not drape pipes all over the sitting-room ceiling and that they put the electric plugs in the right places. Besides, she had some more ideas for improvements while work was in progress, so she was able to have everything done just as she wanted it. The most convenient privy came in very useful, because it took them a long time to dig a cess pit and install a proper lavatory. Camouflage came down from Bowden Farm to live with us. At first she was very frightened of the workmen, but she soon got used to them.

Well, what else is there to tell? Mummy is going to be head

of her department at the Modern school. Daddy is going to buy her a car. I am going to the Grammar school next term. Michael has joined the National Youth Orchestra. The only thing I was sad about was Miss Barnaby. But then even that turned out all right because she went into such a nice home where she has a little flat of her own with a tiny kitchen to cook her own meals, while there are people there to look after her if she is ill. She was able to take some of her own furniture and things from the house in Palace Road, which has been sold, and still gives us tea out of the Rockingham tea service and plays for Michael on her 'cello, when we go to see her. And her great friend from Manchester, the musical one, is going to come and live in the flat next door, so they will be able to talk about music all day long, and it won't matter if the other old ladies talk about Bingo, television and their operations.

And, finally, there is one more thing. Camouflage is a changed character. She no longer, alas, comes for walks with us along No Road for Motors. She has other things to think about.

GLOSSARY

GLOSSARY

Aga—British stove
beck—a small brook
bolted—produced seed prematurely
bullock—a young bull
caravan—a trailer
cooker—a stove on which food is cooked
dry-stone wall—wall constructed of uncemented stone
fell—moor
flags—flagstones
fretted—adorned or embroidered
gill—a narrow valley or ravine
larder—a pantry
loofah—a hard sponge for washing oneself
mac—a raincoat
metalled—paved or macadamized
moithered—bothered
nobbut—only
nowt—nothing
owt—anything
peggy tub—washtub; the peggy is a wooden instrument used to
              beat or stir clothes in the process of washing
pergola—an arbor or trellis
plonging—sinking down suddenly or heavily
post—the mail

prefect—a student monitor
privy—an outhouse or outside toilet
quiff of hair—a whiff or puff of hair
rock bun or cake—a hard bun or cake with a rough surface
R.S.P.C.A.—Royal Society for the Prevention of Cruelty to
          Animals
spate—flood
stretcher—the frame on which canvas is stretched, for painting
summat—something
telly—television set
Wellingtons—rain boots

OTHER BOOKS YOU WILL ENJOY

Lisa, Bright and Dark

John Neufeld

"Just make yourself comfortable and keep talking," M.N. said to Lisa. "Say anything that comes into your head."

But saying that to Lisa Shilling was like asking the ocean, as a favor, to turn cold in February.

For Lisa couldn't help saying anything that came into her head. On her good days, Lisa was as bright and natural as her friends; on her dark days, she was depressed, withdrawn, and deep in conversation with her "English voices."

Lisa Shilling, sixteen, was losing her mind.

M.N. Fickett, the first of Lisa's friends to realize Lisa's dangerous state of mind, is also the first to understand that Lisa's only hope of help must come from her friends. M.N. persuades Betsy Goodman and Elizabeth Frazer that "group therapy" is the answer—providing Lisa with a way of letting off some of the terrific inward pressure, postponing the inevitable explosion.

But Lisa doesn't make their work easy. She's alternately sensible and violent, open and deceitful, clear-headed and confused.

LISA, BRIGHT AND DARK is a novel as current as the last time you looked at your wristwatch. Lisa and her friends are totally real, caring about real things: civil rights, sex, Paul Newman, riots, diet jello, Paul Newman, and their futures.

Funny as young people are, concerned in the same way, determined but a little at sea, Lisa's "doctors" set out on a path of aid and comfort that will cause readers to reflect seriously, smile in recognition, and sympathize totally with Lisa and her illness.

TOUCHING

John Neufeld

Two things happened at once: I saw the Volkswagen bus, and
I began to sweat. It was hot in the airport, and hotter on the
curb. But it wasn't that hot, not even in June. . . .

I walked toward the open doors, ducked my head, kissed
my stepmother, Ellie, hello and saw them. I didn't look directly
at them. I was just conscious they were there: two wheelchairs
locked into the floor of the bus at the back. Two wheelchairs
with two scarecrow figures sitting in them, twisted.

My stepmother slid around in her seat and motioned at
the pair of girls behind her. "This," she said pointing, "is
Twink. And this is one of her friends, Mary Jane. Harry's
here now," she said to them.

I had to look then. Just for a second, I had to look straight
at them. I tried to smile hello before I realized how dumb that
was. Mary Jane's head wasn't turned in my direction, and
Twink couldn't even see.

Then I heard the sounds. Sort of chortles, I guess.
Almost happy sounds.

And then I felt sick.

Harry Walsh, 16, a rather casual "preppie," meets his
stepsister, also 16, for the first time. It rocks him.

And their meeting will shake young readers too. For
Harry's world—careless, easy, typical—is as far as it could be
from Twink's—troubled, painful, and yet worth it all.

John Neufeld has told Twink's story without tears and
flowers, without bright colors and happy endings. It is a gutsy,
sometimes shocking but always real tale of a girl who could
have been forgotten, and wasn't.

THE YEAR

SUZANNE LANGE

For Ann Sanger, the year she spent on an Israeli kibbutz was infinitely more demanding and totally different from the nice neat package of time she had dreamed about in Texas. Eighteen years old, she had left the United States, despite the opposition of her parents, with a group of young Americans and Canadians to help with the work of an Israeli kibbutz near the Syrian border.

Slowly and painfully Ann and her companions learn the necessity for hard work, self-discipline, cooperation, and above all, for tolerance of others different from themselves. Struggling to become useful and respected members of the community they discover in themselves unexpected weaknesses and surprising strengths while in the background hangs the ever present threat of sudden death under the guns of the Arab terrorists across the border.

THE YEAR is a novel of young people, growing and struggling with the realities of a harsh frontier and learning to accept the joys and sorrows of work and play, love and friendship.